A New Dreaming

Ross Bishop

The Truth Will Set You Free

A New Dreaming

Ross Bishop

The Truth Will Set You Free

LIFE SKILLS AUSTRALIA
First published by Life Skills Australia.
(02) 8005 6777. International +61 2 8005 6777.
PO Box 30, Merimbula, New South Wales, 2548. Australia.
www.lifeskillsaustralia.com. Email: info@lifeskillsaustralia.com

© Copyright 2010 Ross Bishop. All rights reserved. Apart from any fair dealing for the purposes of private study, research, criticism or review as permitted under the Copyright Act 1968, no part of this book may be reproduced, stored in a retrieval system, or transmitted in any form or by any means, electronic, mechanical, photocopying, recording or otherwise, without the prior written permission of the Publisher.

National Library of Australia Cataloguing-in-Publication entry
Bishop, Ross.
A new dreaming : the truth will set you free / Ross Bishop.
9780980645262 (pbk.)
A823.4

Design and layout by Life Skills Australia. www.lifeskillsaustralia.com
Printed in USA and UK by Lightning Source Ltd
Printed in Australia by Digital Print Australia

Cover image and back cover image (edited) courtesy of NASA Human Spaceflight Collection. International Space Station Imagery. ISS007-E-10807. 21 July 2003. This view of Earth's horizon as the sunsets over the Pacific Ocean was taken by an Expedition 7 crew member onboard the International Space Station (ISS). http://www.nasaimages.org.

To my Goddess and wife, who has put up with my crazy ways and compulsion to get a greater truth out to the world at large, hence the writing of this fictional book.

Contents

Reflection	1
Introduction	3
Revelation	5
Chapter 1. A Planet of Light	11
Chapter 2. Arrival of the Dark Lord	25
Chapter 3. A Farewell Feast to Remember	33
Chapter 4. Journey to a New Home	41
Chapter 5. A Child of Light is Born	45
Chapter 6. Trials of Initiation	55
Chapter 7. Singar's Return from the Dead	69
Chapter 8. Danger Met with Fire and Light	79
Chapter 9. Change of Role for Singar	89
Chapter 10. Re-Acquaintance with an Old Friend	91
Chapter 11. Final Initiation Rites	103
Chapter 12. Courting Time	117
Chapter 13. Singar's Soul Retreat and Revelation Time	121
Chapter 14. A Great Catastrophe	129
Chapter 15. New Leadership	133
Chapter 16. Singar's Brush with Death	145
About The Author	151

Preface

This book has been written to inspire others to walk and talk their truth and hold fast to the belief that there is good in the world at large.

Acknowledgements

A special thanks to my mother and father who have always supported me with my metaphysical interests, investigations and endeavors.

A very special thanks must go to my editor in chief Carolyn Ward for the time, effort and suggestions she has put forward to magically transform my gibberish into good English prose

Also a thank you is in order for Gabrielle Searant for her contributions, support and input.

I must sincerely thank Matthew Corcoran and Jayne Wood from Life Skills Australia for their professional publishing guidance and wonderful assistance in making this book come to life.

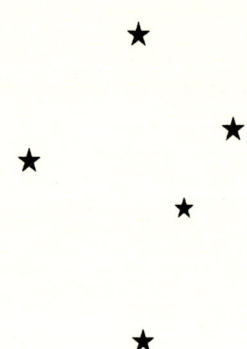

Reflection

Long ago, in a time before man,
came a word and sound that
allowed form to take shape and found
the perfected original harmonic balance
in all facets of nature, trees, birds and Earth.

Man's role was to blend in, to allow each facet
reflect an understanding of life's magnificent plan.
To learn lessons of growth to fulfil a dream,
that some may grow to enlightenment
and just be – be with Me and help
others to do likewise.

Our greatest teachers would be what surrounds
in the perfect physical form; which is an echo of Me.
Alas, we know all too well what has transpired.
A wicked one with only self desires has aspired
to confuse and halt all in their progressive state.
Now this energy has been removed and a
return to My harmonic state of bliss and contentment
can once again take place, in your space.
All is complete for the Goddess to now move
to where I can show her my happy place.
One she has sought for eons of time
and deservedly now can be first to arrive and be.

My signposts are clear, her guidance is near
to now relax and know all will go well.
As many now watch and wait for this knell
a reverberation of glee, will abound as one
has completed her journey and found
My loving embrace on hand to congratulate
this achievement in a place so profound.
It is now time to allow this event to resound
and give all hope that a way exists
out of the valley of trouble and despair
and into the valley of love and delight - what a sight.

Come now in innocence and awe as
you leave behind a shell of a male hell
and find a crystalline bodice to nestle and transform
you to a happy place and one you will enjoy.
As all your love and all your needs will be there
awaiting on beckoned call.
The magic of creating at will that which you need
will be the seed of contentment, joy and to be!

Introduction

A great travesty of justice had prevailed throughout the universe for a very long time. Many had been totally unaware of this conspiracy, which included a deviously disguised program of stalling the soul's progress.

The introduction of progressive containments had effectively shut down the soul's higher sensing capabilities, the soul's intuitive wisdom and the soul's intimate connection with Divine energies.

This masterly stroke of genius was the work of one Dark Lord who had cleverly overseen the phasing in of this scheme over a period of time with the result that souls were now virtually dormant, asleep in a continuous cycle of life and death. They were existing without any real purpose or soul evolvement for thousands of years. The ideal philosophy of soul evolvement back to its source had been forgotten through the mists of time.

All had been forgotten; all had been lost; and eventually all soul's evolvement wisdom was erased from their collective memory – and so the ruse was complete. No soul would now evolve beyond the level of the fallen angels and Dark Lord, who now totally controlled the Karmic cycles of life and death.

However, there was still some hope. A number of special souls were still awake on Terra; they were the special children of the dreaming. They had come from an advanced distant star, for one purpose and one purpose only – to help the people remember.

These children of the dreaming have kept alive the ideal of a happier, peaceful world returning. These children are now collectively sending out dreams to awaken all the sleeping lost souls. Many souls have become receptive again due to vibrational increases in the planets crystalline body. The true meaning of life is again being sensed. The time has arrived, it has been prophesied for centuries – the great awakening begins.

Unfortunately, a growing number of dark beings are now rising up in resistance, resentment and anger at this growing awakening, as they wish to keep things the same for they control many of the larger institutions on Terra. A great battle of wills looms near.

This story begins a long time ago before all this, before the Universe fell into darkness and so this is where we shall begin.

Note: Karrindor travelled from a small planet located in the Alpha Centauri A Star System, however for the purposes of this story the planet was referred to as simply 'Alpha Centauri'.

Revelation

A long time ago, a million or so years ago, periods of time were known as ages and cycles, with seven cycles to an age with each cycle lasting about ten thousand years. This story starts in the first age – third cycle. During this time, all new souls throughout the universe were testing the pristine waters on many planets and experimenting with form and matter.

At this time two beings ruled supreme in their separate halves of the universe. One being was strong, kind, firm yet compassionate and was loved dearly by his people on his home planet of Alpha Centauri.

His name was Karrindor and he had evolved quickly and learned many lessons on the tree of life. However, humility and pride were the two lessons he still grappled with. The other being ruling the other half of the universe, including a planet called Terra, was a self-made leader of cunning and resourcefulness.

His name was Ceramon. He was very intelligent and could see how to use the universal laws to suit his own purpose of total control and ultimate power. He also had been grappling with some of the lessons of life's evolvement, particularly with the male ego and emotional loss of love. He therefore took the easy way out by choosing not to understand them and not to grow with them, but stay stagnant and hold all his half of the universe to his level of evolvement.

He did this by placing holographic and geometric forms containing his energy signatures around the most evolved planets in his half of the universe and other various solar systems. This served his purpose admirably.

One such planet that he wished to hold back was Terra, as it was a very important soul evolvement planet of growth and learning. Hence, a great travesty of justice and free will that allows souls to evolve was lost forever on Terra.

There came a time towards the end of the first age, third cycle, when Ceramon hatched a plan to take control of the whole universe. He was tired of the stronger fluctuating energies coming from the other half of the universe, where his adversary Karrindor ruled.

These pulsating energies would often create unrest within set elements on his controlled planets. People wanted improvement and soul evolvement yet he wished to keep a cap on all this and had to keep inventing false evolvement ideas to keep them happy.

His plan involved going to speak with Karrindor to put forward a proposal that on the surface looked plausible but was steeped in treachery and deceit.

He would attempt to show Karrindor and the people on Alpha Centauri how one of his less evolving planets, Terra, was seemingly lost and going backwards because of radical groups and races that had moved there in earlier times and how they were warring with each other and halting soul evolvement.

He therefore, would seek help to fix these so-called 'problem children' on Terra. He had evidence to show how these radical groups had lost the intimate connection and alignments with the Divine God/Goddess source and, unless they were re-aligned this would eventually lock up all evolving energies throughout the whole universe.

He would impress with his knowledge of the sciences, which he had mastered and point out the concept that we all live in a symbiotic relationship within this universe and use the example of how one bad apple left in a group would soon sour the whole lot.

Ceramon was hoping that his wisdom and philosophy would impress those at the meeting on Alpha Centauri and ensure that they would gladly support his plan. Then once he had the leading lights incarnated on Terra, he would move quickly to totally ensnare them there through great treachery and through hidden containments, thereby locking up these beings to contained and continued cycles of life, death and karmic debts that would be impossible to escape from.

Now the one light being he dearly wished to ensnare was the leader Karrindor, whom he felt would be drawn to this worthwhile cause, as it would also appeal to his ego and pride.

Ceramon worked hard on his evil plot to persuade and convince all of the benefits to his plan. He had despatched ambassadors to Alpha Centauri to start initial dialogue and discussions on his ideas and suggestions. He was so convinced that his plan would work that he started putting in place other futuristic programs that would ensure his control of the whole universe.

One of those initial plans would be to lower the immense light coming from Alpha Centauri. Ceramon was a master of locking in an emotional status or an emotional pain as he had learned how to trap and hold in place any groups emotional pain, thereby locking them into a state of capped emotional understanding and soul growth.

With this evil skill, he hoped to do this to Alpha Centauri once their leader left them and they would descend into a period of grieving for his loss. He would then ensnare it and hold it locked in place.

Ceramon could use the sciences and holographic form to freeze, in situ, an emotional tone and then it would remain in place until someone came along of a higher light frequency than him to unlock it. As most were unaware that the capability existed in the first instance, it would be most unlikely it would ever be shifted.

As he was the brightest light, through guile and cunning, he would prevent anyone from being allowed to rise to his light level or high enough light level to remove this holographic lock.

This practice totally contravened the universal laws and practices, yet Ceramon preyed on people's naivety and innocence to succeed in his ascension to power.

Chapter 1
A Planet of Light

So the day arrived. Karrindor had been awake for some time thinking about this important day and his stirring eventually awoke his long time companion and lover Sarina. "Well, good morning my love. Sorry to awake you, but this day is so important to us all and I could not sleep. How are you feeling?"

Sarina sensed his excitement and intention to probably still go to Terra, even after their many talks and now her resentment towards him flowed strongly. "You know I'm upset and angry at you, so why ask? I cannot believe that you are seriously contemplating agreeing with that snake Ceramon".

Karrindor, realising his mistake in being too buoyant and happy, quickly changed the subject. "Well, we'll see what he offers. Anyway the day is too lovely to ruin with dismay and worry".

This dismissal of her by Karrindor only served to upset her more. "Kar (as she fondly referred to him as) do not avoid me so. I beg you – do not go on this crazy mission. Our people will not manage without you".

Sarina was extremely anxious for Alpha Centauri's future and well-being. She again tried her best to make him see reason yet her words were falling on deaf ears.

Karrindor was anxious to get the day underway and replied, "I know you are angry and upset with me but we do not have time to discuss it any further now, for we have work to do in preparation for the visiting delegation arriving from Sirius later today. Please go about your business and we will talk later".

Sarina was hurt and worried and left in a hurry for she loved Karrindor and wished him to remain on Alpha Centauri with her. Karrindor was gifted with abundant love and as such, she was aware that their evolving planet was guided and uplifted by this pure love.

While regretting the argument and unresolved grievance, Karrindor was more preoccupied with the activities of the day. Many thoughts raced through his mind pertaining to what still needed to be resolved.

He had taken care of the leadership aspects for his planned absence and felt sure his beloved planet would continue to grow and prosper until his return.

Karrindor knew that if the other half of the universe could not correct its downward spiral, then this would in time, impact adversely on his half of the universe. As well, there existed a symbiotic relationship of sorts.

There was an old agreement he had signed with Ceramon regarding the rights and privileges of each leader and universal segments in relation to trade and growth. It was this interwoven fabric of union that held both together with a common goal of evolvement as the universe was not cut in two or separate aspects but truly one and one only.

Karrindor left his bed and started to wash and dress for the day in his regal attire. He was in the prime of his life at about seventy winter cycles old and wondered how long people lived on Terra. Physical souls on Alpha Centauri lived for about two hundred winters due to the rejuvenating minerals and metals found on their planet and within the five neighbouring star systems.

Karrindor quickly exited his expansive room and headed for the administration and justice building where he was to carry out some last minute discussions with his advisors before the delegation arrived from Sirius. It was not long before his dear friend and planetary ambassador Arkanin, caught up with him. "Lord Karrindor please may we talk?"

"Forget the formalities my dear friend, it is just us two. I also sense your resentment about me going, but please can we work together as one and not argue on this any further."

Arkanin once again felt his emotions surface strongly about losing his long-term friend and leader and he would not be put off from voicing his opinion to dissuade Karrindor from going. "You know this is madness, look what you are leaving behind. Have you no sense of service and loyalty to our planet? Who will rule when you're gone?"

Karrindor held himself in check for a while and then said, "My friend stop, stop now, I have made up my mind to go, so please, work with me and not against me. As far as the matter of leadership is concerned, I have appointed a body of leaders to rule in my absence, four men including you Arkanin and three women who will act as the ruling advisory body.

You will all work in harmony with the council of elders who have much wisdom to offer. They are to be consulted on any major development you decide to undertake. Now let us conclude our proposal and make it foolproof and without fault for I do not fully trust my counterpart Ceramon and his intention.

I will journey to this planet and limit myself to three incarnations in an attempt to realign their thinking and get them back on track and then return home. Who knows Arkanin, you may still be around as an elder when I return."

Somewhere deep within Arkanin, an ominous feeling told him it would possibly be the opposite and he would be losing a close friend for a long time.

Karrindor then withdrew to himself and spent time fine-tuning his personal skills, which would be his secret reservoir of capabilities to take with him. Without Ceramon knowing, he would lock these into his cellular memory via his six basic origin cells (those that go with you from lifetime to lifetime). This way he could access them at will during his incarnations on Terra.

The skills and capabilities he knew how to use included: levitation; using harmonic sound resonance for moving heavy objects and building purposes; unconditional love, compassion and a soul love of his planet, reciprocated by the planet; healing with crystals and minerals; a musical voice that would calm the most troubled minds; and an ability to connect into intra-planetary alignments and draw on the energies of his own planet, which included the magical mystical powers of Alpha Centauri.

Alpha Centauri was indeed a planet of unity and power.

A musical/hypnotic power shield could be created whenever the planet was threatened by alien forces: with all the people joining like minds, an etheric shield would be created and projected out around the planet as a strong defensive beam. Then the elders would ascertain the nature of the threat and decide on whether an interception was necessary or allow the craft to enter if it was deemed friendly. The planetary shield was so powerful it would stop and neutralize any incoming ship and hold it in suspended animation until a decision was made on the visitor's intentions.

As well, Karrindor would take with him the skill and knowledge of summoning the elements of Earth, Fire, Water and Air, plus the ability to meld and work with these elements quickly and easily.

These essences and gifts of skill would surely arm him with enough capabilities to assist those lost souls on Terra and help them see their way clear from darkness and back into the light.

All he had learnt through his evolvement on Alpha Centauri would now serve to remind him of his heritage and origin, as, when you descend into lower dimensional fields, you tend to lose memory and sensitivity to life's meaning and opportunities. He knew that through each cycle of birth, death and reincarnation one lost all conscious memory of past incarnations. Yet these could always be recalled through deep mediation and accessing the higher conscious mind aspects of ones being.

Sometimes blockages in ones chakras due to pain or suffering are encountered, therefore hindering greatly the ability to recall past learning. Karrindor, however, had a plan to use his ancillary sensing tool (his moon chakra – at the lower back of the head) in order to always be able to access his true higher consciousness.

He expected to find most of the people on Terra with either blocked chakras or they simply would not be fully awakened due to their limited spiritual growth. He believed he could help them quickly awaken to the truths available through connecting to their own Higher Consciousness.

Karrindor was going to agree to three incarnations on this far off planet and request angelic support on his spiralling descent into form and matter in this other realm. He was optimistic that he could do this quickly and then return home to Alpha Centauri where their evolvement could continue again; at present it was held back by the lack of progress in the other half of the Universe.

He thought he would miss his home planet because of its peace, tranquillity and happiness but he felt it was his duty to somehow help save this other half of the known Universe. He hoped the sacrifice would be worth it in the end.

Karrindor loved the healing mineral thermal pools that he had helped create on Alpha Centauri. One was beneficial to those who needed soul aligning, healing and sustenance, while the sister pool helped heal the emotional hurts of the heart. He wondered if anything like this was available down on Terra.

As Karrindor continued to reflect on his life full of contentment and satisfaction, he hoped he could find this as well on this new planet. Then he heard the call of his faithful pet Mintor, who had been looking for him. He seldom was far from his master except when he went hunting for skien, his favourite food (a mouse-like creature). Karrindor wondered if Mintor would like to come with him on this exciting journey and incarnate into one of the animals on Terra in the hope it would be a reminder of home for him. He would also be a great companion in a foreign land.

Karrindor still remembered the day he found Mintor out on the grassy plains as a funny fur ball running and playing with the insects that were prevalent at that time of the year.

Mintor, known as a caving, showed no fear of Karrindor as he approached. This was very unusual and Karrindor thought that it may have thought him a big insect and wanted to play with him. He just looked at Karrindor with those big brown innocent eyes for a long time and then settled down beside him. He claimed Karrindor then and there as his new master.

Karrindor thought that this fur ball must have become separated from his litter and although he searched far and wide that day, he could not find the rest of his litter or family. He therefore decided to temporarily take this little creature home and care for him until he became strong enough to be released back into the wild.

A strong bond formed between Karrindor and the little caving, who he decided to call Mintor because it meant 'no fear' and he became a very devoted pet. Mintor was like no animal that currently existed on Terra – he was something between a cat, dog and a monkey and was highly intelligent and loved to climb trees.

Mintor could sense a threat or danger well before any mortal could. Mintor, in the past had warned Karrindor of approaching alien spacecraft and Karrindor always knew by his wail that danger was imminent. In this way, the originator of the planetary warning signal was often Mintor. Once the threat was intuitively sensed and evaluated by the wise ones, the all clear would be given and the protective shield would be lowered to allow in the visiting spacecraft.

On this day as Karrindor patted his devoted companion, Mintor suddenly started his strong wail of warning and the precautionary measures were put in place to ascertain the nature of the threat. Karrindor expected it to be the visiting ambassadors from the planet, Sirius A and their sector ruler Ceramon and as such no real threat at all. Nevertheless, he did wonder inwardly if this was some omen and a true warning by Mintor.

As Karrindor anticipated, the wise ones, through astral projection, eventually gave the all clear as they perceived the imminent arrival of the ambassador's party, which included one large ship and two smaller military escort ships.

Karrindor summoned his advisors and sent a message via his servants to the kitchen staff to start preparing the banquet for their visitors. He sent a message to Sarina, his mistress, to also prepare herself to receive the visiting dignitaries.

Karrindor knew that this would be a difficult meeting, with much bargaining and would go on until both parties were happy with their desired outcomes.

Karrindor thought some more on the capabilities he should be allowed to take with him and wanted absolute assurance that they would agree to his terms and conditions. He would be coming under the local jurisdiction of Sirius A, as it was the more advanced and guiding planet in Terra's half of the Universe and, as such, he would need support from their ruling priests, who would have come here with Ceramon. The last time he had met priests from Sirius A they seemed to be totally under the spell of Ceramon. He thought it would be interesting to see how they behaved this time.

He had heard that the Sirians were a very war like people and were very strict and severe in their demeanour and manners. However, this was not uncommon amongst lower evolving planets. He had witnessed this before on planets, within his ruling half of the universe. Karrindor had visited some of these evolving planets a few years ago in one of his own ships, when he had set out to create friendships and expand trade between planets in his region of the Universe.

The beings of these evolving planets were making the same mistakes those on Alpha Centauri had made early on in their growth and although he could see a better way for them, he knew not to interfere in their own learning process. His role was simply to offer help and assistance where necessary.

All souls on Alpha Centauri were taught the Universal Laws at an early age and part of those laws included allowing all souls to evolve at their own pace and in a free will environment, without control or domination.

While Karrindor awaited the arrival of the visiting dignitaries, he reflected on his part in introducing the Universal Laws at appropriate levels for the children to understand initially and then put into practice as they grew up. Whilst waiting, he went through all ten of them mentally in his mind:

- Love is the highest vibrational force in the Universe and holds all matter in form and harmony
- All souls have free will to evolve at their own pace and without any containment
- Honour and respect the oneness, unity and symbiotic relationship between all living creatures, people and planets

- Honour and respect the perfect balance and harmony of both sexes
- Every soul to honour and respect each other as equals and allow freedom of purpose, direction and intent
- Each soul to share any excess and not harbour, steal or horde possessions unnecessarily
- Souls to understand envy and jealousy - to thus allow love, learning and partnerships to grow without constraint for each other's mutual benefit and the learning of life's lessons and evolvement
- Justice, truth and liberty for all souls to be preserved and honoured, Karmic debts to be resolved as soon as possible
- All souls are encouraged to work within the fabric of the Divine Plan and Divine Timing for the highest good of all. (Interestingly, this law, if understood properly, allows much more freedom and opportunity than if you lived otherwise)
- All souls rights to total freedom, joy, peace, happiness, abundance and contentment to be respected at all times

Karrindor knew the Universal laws very well. He was part of an expanding awareness program of goodwill that his ambassadors had passed on to planets throughout the half of the Universe that he governed and protected.

There had been groups of raiding ships in his vicinity of the universe in recent times. Most of these renegade ships carried Reptoids from planets on the outer rim of his nearest Galaxy. They sought to block progress and planetary evolvement by creating fear through harassment, so that their primitive life forms could catch up emotionally to the rest of the advanced Universe.

In recent times, a growing uneasiness had crept in from the other half of the Universe controlled by Ceramon. Karrindor was therefore interested in ascertaining, in the forthcoming meeting, if the other half of the universe were being taught the Divine Universal Laws and Truths, for he suspected that something was not right or the laws were being misinterpreted somehow.

He also wished to ascertain if the Reptoid raiders had penetrated into the other half of the universe where Ceramon ruled, for they were very intelligent and a difficult adversary to hold at bay.

Chapter 2
Arrival of the Dark Lord

With great fanfare, the visiting interplanetary body was announced and proceeded to enter the throne room. They were led by Ceramon, who was his charismatic self, with smiles and gestures, showing respect and honour to Karrindor as the rightful leader in this domain.

"Greetings again, Lord Karrindor" said Ceramon. "It is indeed a pleasure and privilege to be back on your beautiful planet and to once again enjoy your overgenerous hospitality".

The words seemed laced in false praise, yet Karrindor answered, "You are welcome Emperor Ceramon. Thank you for your kind words. I now formally welcome you and your accompanying dignitaries, including the ruling Priests and leaders of Sirius A. Please make yourself welcome during your stay here, now, please sit and enjoy some light refreshments before we get down to the business at hand."

Ceramon then said, "I would like to introduce Cleric Dinsdorm who is the head priest of Sirius A and his council members".

At that instant, one of the Priests stood and nodded, to which Karrindor acknowledged.

Cleric Dinsdorm spoke, "It is a pleasure to meet you Lord Karrindor. We have heard so much about your efforts to improve planetary growth in this region of the Universe. My fellow priests and I are all following a pathway of growth that embodies the sciences and Universal Truths."

Karrindor thought that he must learn more about these specific sciences later on, but not now.

The tension in the room seemed to evaporate as they got to know one other. Karrindor introduced his five planetary advisers who had arrived at the same time as the visitors. More protocol and gifts were exchanged as a measure of good will between respective leaders and dignitaries.

Once this was over, Karrindor stood and said, "My lords and priests, we have prepared a great feast for your arrival, but first may I suggest we get down to the business of discussing what you believe can be done about the slow progress of this recalcitrant planet called Terra. Then we can eat".

Arkanin (as the diplomatic advisor for Alpha Centauri) then took the floor. "Distinguished leaders, we are at a loss to understand why, with great leaders such as yourselves guiding this planet, it refuses to progress. We are also very disturbed that you may attempt to lure our beloved leader into trying to save

Terra, when you seem unable to do anything yourselves".

This was a deliberate attempt by Arkanin to get this visiting group on the back foot and not think they would lure Karrindor there so easily (and at the very least it was an attempt to keep his great friend here on their home planet).

There was a hushed silence for some time before Ceramon spoke, "We acknowledge the comments by the head of the diplomatic core on Alpha Centauri. Yet, we wish you to know that, although what you say seems feasible, we have tried many ways to influence this wayward planet positively. Yet, they continue to ignore our attempts to help them".

This was a good diplomatic reply by Ceramon. He was showing all his guile and cunning as a leader in slowly convincing the gathering that they had truly done their best on Terra. However, the advisors on Alpha Centauri were not going to let Ceramon off lightly and pressured him to reveal fully what they had actually tried on this planet to help it evolve.

The meeting progressed with intensity and the discussion became heated as both sides put forward suggestions. Karrindor's advisors were adamant that a solution could be found without him having to incarnate on this backward planet.

When the tempo faltered slightly, Ceramon again came out with another convincing statement. "Many enlightened souls have already gone to Terra to try and reverse its downhill spiral. Yet in the dense energies there, most lost their direction and purpose and had done little to help. Hence, our last resort was to seek your help and suggest that one of your advanced souls may wish to try and help, maybe even Lord Karrindor himself may like this tempting challenge".

Immediately, there was a great cry and much uproar from the local diplomats, as they witnessed the smooth seduction techniques attempted by this crafty manipulator. The local elders became incensed with this blatant attempt to seduce their leader, some even got up and were preparing to walk out, when Karrindor silenced the gathering and spoke, "What if I decided to accept your offer? What guarantees would I be given to safely return to my beloved planet if I should fail as well; for it seems the will of the Gods at present that this planet remain where it is".

This was a desperate attempt by Karrindor to reassure his followers that he would not be so easily lured there. However, inwardly his ego was excited by this challenge and he did not want to look like he was an easy push over.

The head priest, Dinsdorm, then spoke to the gathering, "We will grant total protection for Lord Karrindor if he chooses to help us. We will also support him by sending an advanced soul from our own planet who would act as a guide for him until he acclimatizes to the energies on this planet".

This reassurance seemed to appease and calm the gathering somewhat, as this showed obvious respect for the leader of Alpha Centauri.

Yet Ceramon sensed that he still needed to offer more bargaining gifts and prospects to win the day. As such, he made his 'coup de grah' statement, "We will put in place a most comprehensive rescue plan to evacuate Lord Karrindor, in the unlikely event that he somehow loses his way.

This can include three of your nominated personnel here on Alpha Centauri. This is evidence that we believe we will never succeed unless we have a great leader like Lord Karrindor to show the people on Terra the way back to the correct pathway of evolving light".

This offer seemed genuine enough with Karrindor declaring, "You do seem genuine with this offer, but we all now need time to eat and reflect. Let us conclude for now and resume after the banquet for it has been ready and prepared for some time now."

As they all walked to the banquet hall, Karrindor quickly found Ceramon and quietly said to him, "Your word of honour sir, on your offer so far, is what I need now".

Ceramon quickly answered, "Yes, you have it".

From this point on it was difficult for Ceramon to contain himself. He knew inwardly that he had won and Lord Karrindor was going to take the bait. He worked very hard to hide his excitement throughout the ensuing dinner.

Karrindor, on the other hand, used the walk to mentally revisit the previous meeting and quickly summarised his reactions to what had transpired; they seemed desperate to win his support and were conceding ground by wild offers of assistance if he should need it on Terra.

In not showing his open keenness to go, he had opened the way for many more concessions being granted to him than he had originally hoped for. As such, he should be able to take many tools of psychic wisdom and skills with him in order to be successful and complete his mission quickly.

He had already decided to make public the announcement of his decision at the formal dinner later that evening and start the official support program of helping Terra; this would, in turn also allow Alpha Centauri to continue to move on further into the Light.

He hoped his people would understand his decision and not think harshly of him. He knew one who would not be happy – Sarina, his partner and companion, but this he could not help. He was after all, making a sacrifice for the highest good of all. Surely, she would eventually understand this.

Too soon, Karrindor had arrived at the banquet, unable to ponder his decision any longer. The finer details would be discussed after the beautiful supper when the visiting dignitaries should be more agreeable.

Chapter 3
A Farewell Feast to Remember

Many were seated in the huge hall and dressed beautifully in the flowing and bright colours of this planet. When the delegation entered all stood to acknowledge respect for the visitors. The guests were guided to their seats and Karrindor immediately noticed the absence of Sarina. He knew he would have to go and search for her.

With a hushed quiet, a bell was rung and food appeared, as if by magic, ushered in by many kitchen staff and servants. Karrindor made the formal introductory announcements of welcoming the leaders of the distant planets and urged all to enjoy the meal and entertainment at hand.

Karrindor then excused himself to search for Sarina. He questioned the assistants who were organising the banquet and finally one said that she had been seen going to the healing garden at the back of the building and had not returned. He quickly found his way there and found a weeping Sarina. After a hushed silence, Karrindor slowly went over to her. He just held her tenderly, allowed the sobs to subside and waited for her to speak first.

"Thank you for coming to find me. I felt our union and bond and our planet's wellbeing were worth more than this silly mission you wish to go on. You have always been the same, ready to jump into the next challenge without thought for others, so please understand that although I am very upset, I will support you now in front of our visiting delegates – only because you request this of me."

Karrindor was dumbfounded by her submission and cooperative change of heart and did not waste any time saying, "Thank you my love – I do appreciate this support though I know it is against your wish and will, but believe me when I say that I have thought long and hard about this and the decision has been incredibly difficult. I didn't want to leave you behind, but my inner guidance keeps saying that this is what I must do, so please forgive me".

With this mutual understanding and the love they felt for each other, they kissed and went hand in hand into the banquet to greet the people, although Sarina was still half-hoping Karrindor might change his mind.

Ceramon (the deceiver) was inwardly happy with the progress of the meeting so far and even felt that a resolution may be forthcoming at tonight's banquet. He reflected on the many other leading lights from other planets that he and his persuasive group of priests had managed to convince to go to Terra and how all of these are now held captive thanks to his countless ensnarements and false karmic debts.

His grand plan of halting all light evolvement throughout the universe was very near to completion. He was now close to the greatest prize of all, Lord Karrindor, the leader of the brightest and most progressive planet in the universe. He thought that he must keep himself in check and not look overly enthusiastic or happy, not yet anyway.

A subdued atmosphere greeted Karrindor and Sarina as they entered the banquet hall. All was quiet as many sensed a foreboding and change of their idyllic lifestyle and future. They sensed their beloved leader was seriously contemplating a dangerous mission to another planet and they were all afraid of what was to come.

Karrindor sensed all their fears and thoughts, as he had learned to do this over time and knew that he needed to say something soon to lift the mood of the crowd. Sarina looked beautiful as usual beside Karrindor. Although tonight, there was a sadness in her eyes perceived by many of the locals, particularly the women.

Next to Karrindor, on his right, sat his faithful advisors and further to his left beyond Sarina sat the visiting delegations who were trying to lighten the mood and make people feel happy about their future and the safety of their leader.

Ceramon was having great difficulty containing himself, as he knew inwardly he had won and was being rather loud and obnoxious, even though he tried to not show his delight too much.

Towards the end of the meal a small group of musicians came in and with a nod from Karrindor, they all started to play the national song of the heart, which united all Alpha Centauri in brotherhood and unity. Karrindor found it difficult to find full voice because of the circumstances and so did many others; which is contrary to what normally happens when this song is played.

Karrindor contemplated singing another song by himself but quickly thought otherwise. Even though he was an accomplished singer in his own right, he was not in the mood and instead stood and addressed his people, "Beloved family, friends and loved ones of Alpha Centauri, I know and sense a lot of you are worried about my decision and so I felt that now was the opportune time to tell you of my decision which I have not made lightly or without a great deal of deliberation and counsel. Yet there appears to be really only one answer.

Since this proposal was first put to me by Lord Ceramon five moons ago, I have thought long and hard on it. If what they say is true, then on this single planet called Terra lies an answer to the progress of the whole universe. I therefore will not hold you in suspense any longer for I have decided to go (background sighs, weeps and sounds of 'Ah no' could be heard, while the visiting delegation clapped wildly)."

Karrindor waited for the room to quieten once again and continued, "I will depart tomorrow with these visitors. I ask for your support and understanding. I have left our planet in capable hands (Karrindor looked towards his loyal advisors and wise ones) so all should continue as before. Please understand that I feel it is my duty to go and help – I love you all".

Light applause started through hand clapping, most of which was coming from the visiting delegation.

At the end of the meal, Karrindor was able to catch up with one of the visiting priests as planned. He learned that Reptoid Raiders had also arrived in their part of the Universe and in fact had established colonies on some of their isolated planets.

This was disturbing news indeed and maybe cause for some of the problems on Terra. He did not have time to discuss the Universal Laws at length, but some misunderstandings did seem evident to him.

After the banquet, the final arrangements were made by both parties. Ceramon contained himself by appearing to give-in begrudgingly to each of Lord Karrindor's requests for skills and capabilities to be taken with him, designed to assist him with his goal of persuasion and realigning the people on Terra.

Karrindor's' guidance from the Elders also saw him initiate a plan to isolate and sever any unnecessary attachments that might occur between him and the Sirian woman that he was to be paired with for his mission down on Terra. This request was also accepted. The polarity balance on Terra required a strong woman to balance and support Karrindor in a twin-soul management plan. (This was a local custom that needed following.)

That evening, nothing he could say or do would placate Sarina. He withdrew to his private den to contemplate and reflect on all that had transpired to make sure he had not missed anything. He felt confident about everything. If he should fail, there was even a rescue plan in place to extricate him as a last resort.

Before retiring, he packed a simple bag, mainly to get him to Sirius A and to cover the few days there before the incarnation process would begin. Part of him was excited by the adventure, yet another deeper part was concerned that something was not quite right. As he packed, he tried to throw off his doubts and focus on the journey ahead.

He wondered about the people of Terra: what colour they were; what size they were; how long they lived for. As his trip would take about five days in duration, he aimed to find out a lot more about these people during this time. As tiredness eventually overcame him he retired to an empty cold bed and succumbed to a restless sleep.

Chapter 4
Journey to a New Home

And so began an odyssey for Karrindor and his faithful pet Mintor, who refused to be left behind. Everyone had agreed that Mintor would be good company down on Terra and serve to remind him of his past. It was well known that travel into denser energy fields often resulted in loss of memory of any previous incarnations and one's purpose in life.

Now, this soul reincarnation of Karrindor on planet Terra would take more than the few lifetimes his people had been led to believe. It would, in fact, last 753,000 years, for he would become ensnared and trapped by the greatest deception plan ever created in all history.

The time on Sirius A was short but busy, as a recipient had been found down on Terra who was ready to have a child. Karrindor's soul therefore needed to be quickly prepared for this transition.

He remembered that he never felt at ease or at all comfortable on Sirius A. It seemed such a severe place with strict rules and procedures governing all aspects of life. There did not appear to be any freedom, laughter or excitement anywhere. He presumed that it might be lighter out in the country: but little did Karrindor know that the priests had total control of the people and ruled with a strong disciplinary, even dictatorial manner on this planet.

It was this type of hierarchal rule that also flowed on to Terra, as they were the chosen guardians and caretakers on Terra under Ceramon's rule. Karrindor also met the chosen Sirian woman who would be a soul polarity match for him down on Terra. She seemed quiet, polite and yet plain in appearance with a reserved demeanour. She seemed to sense in this outsider a chance for her to improve and evolve further, although her motives were indeed more selfish and insular than those of Karrindor's.

Karrindor was a lot taller than most of the people on Sirius A and only a few priests were close to his height. He therefore spent a great deal of time ducking his head as he traversed the many rooms the priests guided him through; a necessity for his adjustment process. He was told that the race of people he would incarnate into would be a primitive native North American tribe that had good structure and potential for growth.

Soon Karrindor, the woman from Sirius and Mintor were put to sleep and astrally aligned to the worm hole inflow energies and, through a long thin tunnel connected (like a star gate) to a reception point down on Terra, for instantaneous travel. This process also lowered their light energy resonance to be similar to the light energy field down on Terra.

This dream state passage seemed slow to Karrindor. Eventually he remembered looking down on a lovely planet, with much blue water abounding and some very green landmasses. It did look very inviting and not totally unlike his home planet, with about 80% of the planet being covered in water.

He remembered little else until some time later when he looked around and realised his female companion was missing. Karrindor was told that his Sirian female companion had already incarnated into a tribe near where he was soon to be born.

The two advisers from Terra then continued to explain how his absorption into the planets cycle of life and death would take place and how and where he would arrive. They also reviewed some customs and behaviour from this planet that seemed very cruel and backward to him. However, by understanding that it was a slow and low vibrational planet, he realised that he might encounter some unusual behaviours. As well he felt that everything was virtually standing still and he was eager to start his incarnation.

The time finally arrived when Karrindor knew a new beginning would take place, as he had been shown his future mother and she looked very pregnant indeed.

Chapter 5
A Child of Light is Born

As a child born into a 'Sons of Chiefs' line, this baby was very welcome. He not only ensured the survival of the line of chiefs but also, as he was a first born, he had claims to one day be the chief of the tribe.

He was given the name of Singar, meaning 'Light One', reflecting his light build compared to most of the other robust children born in this tribe. Although his father, Hawk, accepted his light build, he hoped he would soon fatten up under his mother's nurturing.

Singar's mother's name was Kara and she adored this first born child of hers, even if he was slight of build and didn't cry as much or as loud as all the other babies did.

After a while, both parents sensed deep down that this child was different somehow from the other children. Singar often spoke from a level of understanding well beyond his years and from a very young age seemed much more alert and engaging, sensing what needed to be done ahead of time.

Childhood to boyhood happened quickly for Singar and his mother, who was besotted with her loving son. He showed her much affection and helped her with many of the chores, such as gathering wood and setting fires, making her life much easier. Kara also knew that she should not pamper him too much. Being first born he needed to run with the other boys and learn to stand up for himself and find a place amongst the pack of youths who were already sorting out leaders and pecking orders.

For this reason, she would often say, "Singar you've helped me enough today, go and run with the other boys".

Much of the time Kara worried about him as he was so different. She feared for his future and his ability to fit into the role of chief male protector and provider in the dynamics of the tribe. Singar always sensed his mothers urging and would head off towards the other boys. At the last minute he would dart into the forest where he loved to roam by himself.

Singar grew up quickly and was wise beyond his years showing a mature understanding of human frailty. He seemed to not care or worry as much about life as most of those around him did. He seemed to know instinctively that all things happen for a reason and that lessons were meant to be learnt from these events. This was not always welcome advice from someone as young and small as Singar, so, as time went by, he learned to keep his mouth shut rather than offer a solution.

Although tall and lean, he was by no means weak, for he carried out his allocated duties with ease and efficiency. He could then go exploring amongst nature in the forests. Often during these wanderings, he would become lost in time with his excitement and the beauty of the forest. He would come home late and receive a scalding from Kara, who worried about not having seen him around for most of the day.

In the forest, he knew when animals trusted him although he sensed their initial nervousness towards him. In time they all learned to trust him. As well, the trees and elements all seemed to reach out to him and he became one with everything around him: in true harmony with it all.

Singar was also interested in what the women did; what bulbs and food supplements they would use in the cooking pots to provide taste and health nourishment and what healing herbs they would search for to tend the sick or elderly, or for use during child birth.

He found this a lot more interesting than running with the other boys, who only wanted to test him and challenge him to a duel, a race or a dare. Courage inspired respect in the Indian tribe, which finally resulted in one being accepted as a brave.

Sadly, Singar was seen by all as a misfit and was only tolerated because he was of the line of "Sons of Chiefs". At one point his father had to stand up for his son and ask that he not be banished and be given more time to grow and learn. This would allow him to at least attempt the initiation trials at 11 summers old like all the other youths.

Deep down, he knew that this unusual son of his was special. He needed to establish what it was about Singar that would benefit the tribe and save him from exile or death, for weakness was not tolerated in this tribe.

It was strength and courage that had saved them many times from the arch enemy across the rift canyon – the Chitzuang and Black Sioux tribes. Fighting over tribal and hunting lands had kept them warring for too long. There was hope that one day there would be peace again, probably not in his lifetime, unfortunately; but maybe in Singar's.

A new life came to the family unit when Singar was seven summers old. Kara had nearly given up hope of another child. This child was a boy, named Hook, who cried a lot and took all of his mother's attention, as a result Singar found himself further alienated from his mother. His father didn't want him hanging around as much either as he was busy with his chores repairing tepees, providing clothes to help his family and attending to his hunting tools.

Singar was left once again to befriend the young women who were allocated wood duties, fire duties, cooking and cleaning duties and making new clothes and coats for winter. They tolerated Singar, for he was pleasant and asked many questions. However, they never considered him a future mate because he was not strong and courageous like all the other braves: to them, he seemed weak, effeminate and so different.

One summer's day Singar had secretly crept out and followed a group of young women to the river for washing. It was a beautiful day and everything seemed to be reaching out and touching him. The smell of the beautiful green grasses and country was so invigorating and uplifting for him.

On this day, a group of older boys also came down to the riverbanks to where Singar was conversing with the young squaws (girls who were about to come into contractual marriage age) and witnessed the strange behaviour of this youth working with them. They had heard of his soft and feminine ways and it angered them that he was not showing signs of being a brave and playing with the boys of his age.

Suddenly, Singar understood what it was to feel fear. They approached and told the squaws not to talk to him and to leave him immediately. One grabbed Singar and said, "I think you need a washing as well'.

The older boy dragged him to the river and, being a big, strong lad, he easily pushed Singar into the river at a deep point – he went under and seemed to stay there for a long time believing his lungs would burst.

Finally, he reached the surface to the laughter of this group of youths. The same large brave then threw Singar further out into the river. It was then that he felt a new sensation; a primordial deep surge of energy started to bubble up within him. He had not felt this before and it propelled him along with the current and helped him reach shore a lot further downstream. He had swallowed a lot of water though and with heavy wet clothes, weighing him down he had just enough energy to crawl up the bank before retching and throwing up out of both fear and shock. He noticed that only then, did this protective elevated energy field around him subside and soon he fell asleep exhausted.

Waking at the setting sun, feeling very cold and hungry, his initial response was one of panic – but then, once again, this calmness and strange protective energy field came over him. He relaxed and knew instinctively which way to go to find his camp, even though it was hard to see in the growing darkness.

Singar did not know then, but he had connected to the collective group energy field of earth, trees, nature and elements.

His mother was initially furious with him for once again staying out this late. She scolded him seriously and told him to see his father immediately.

Singar knew the other boys would have talked and he would be in trouble for being with the women and not practising to be a brave. He saw his father talking to his grandfather, the chief, whose name was Two Rivers. They were talking in serious tones and he felt this was a bad omen. He approached and waited to be called forward.

Hawk saw his son nearby but waited until the chief had expressed his dismay at what he had heard about Singar from some of the other families. He was deliberating what to do with Singar as it seemed he was becoming a liability to the tribe and causing friction.

Once again Hawk stood up for his son and said, "Father let him go in the initiation trials tomorrow and let that be our guide as to his fate".

He hoped somehow, that some miracle would happen to save Singar from a fate of tribal expulsion.

Reluctantly, Two Rivers agreed, as he beckoned Singar forward and spoke sternly to him. He did, however, sense that Singar was looking very unwell and not himself at all and said, "You have been chosen to go through the boys' initiation rites of passage to brave status and you will leave with the other boys tomorrow".

Hawk then spoke to Singar, "I will speak to you later. Go now and help with the evening meal".

Singar wearily trudged to his tepee and asked what he could do. As everything had been done already he simply ate what broth and dried meat his mother put out for him. He was drifting off to sleep under a warm fur-skin when his father awoke him with a firm shake. "Singar, what happened today? Tell me!"

Feeling shamed, Singar related the whole story to his father – leaving out the strange feeling of power and energy that surged through him at a time of desperation.

His father only nodded and then proceeded to tell Singar that a serious situation had developed. This last incident was the final straw in a series of embarrassing situations Singar had found himself in and so now he was being given one last chance to prove himself as a brave or possibly face banishment from the tribe. Hawk then silently said that he wished his son well and may the Great Spirit protect and guide him.

Singar started to plan ahead and had already thought to take his best knife, quiver, bow and arrows that he had secretly been given by his father to hopefully stimulate his keenness in becoming a hunting brave. Singar thought the weapons looked appealing, even pretty but he did not want to hurt any animals as they were all his friends. He would take them any way to please his father.

He then fell asleep thinking about what he had been told of these initiation rites – five days alone in the bush around the next mountain range. It would take the elders one day to lead them to their starting point, were they would be left on their own to find shelter and food and keep warm by whatever means they could.

If they survived these five days, they would then have to pass a basic elders quiz on tribal lore – which seemed simple enough. "May the Great Spirit guide and protect me", was his last thought before sleep took him.

Chapter 6
Trials of Initiation

At sunrise the sounds of early activity in the camp could be heard with the extra excitement of this initiation day. Apparently, some of the young girls would also go through a secret women's initiation rite to prove they were fit and ready to mate with a brave.

Singar donned his leather clothes and moccasins to protect him on his walk through the rough bush and quickly left the tepee to greet the rising sun. He overheard two braves discussing how they could be in danger taking part in such an early initiation rite, as some of the older bears were still in the mountains feeding off the last of the red berries that were common to the area.

Some felt the occasion should be postponed a while, but the chief vetoed this. Immediately after this trial, the camp would move to their winter home. They needed to be well stocked with various food types, buffalo hides and animal skins to see out the freezing winter.

They set out, seven boys in all, mostly 11 or 12 summers old, yet Singar was only 10 summers old.

Although not much smaller in height then most of them, he was certainly a lot thinner as he hadn't filled out as much as the other youths.

The walking was easy and enjoyable, for although no one spoke, each youth was anxious for this trial to begin and be completed successfully. This would mean they would then be respected and recognised as a brave in training, ready to ride with other men in hunting expeditions and in providing for the tribe as a whole – so a sense of urgency prevailed with the walkers as the destination was now in sight.

As they walked briskly, Singar was excited about being selected to do these trials and he said quietly to himself that he would not disappoint or embarrass his father again. His mind also drifted to when the bullies had dumped him in the river and unfortunately, some of these youths were also on this initiation trial. Singar decided he would try to stay well out of their way.

He also thought about this strange energy feeling he had experienced during the near drowning event in the river. Since that time, he had quietly sat amongst nature and tried to draw in that energy again, sometimes he had succeeded which was exciting and felt good.

Often during these quiet times he would have glimpses of a far away happy place that was vaguely familiar yet still elusive. This place and space gave him a sense of knowing that all life was connected and something beautiful held it all in harmony. During these times of peaceful meditation, he saw something small dancing around everything like the wind. Instinctively, he knew that these small creatures that danced around him could be controlled and he would feel warm and a small breeze would flow around him.

Singar knew he had stumbled upon something very important and looked forward to doing more experimenting with these dancing, very small energy lights, while he was on these trials. He seemed to only see them vaguely when in a deeply relaxed state, almost an altered state of reality and he saw them as layers over the top of all living things - animals and trees. This was like a great discovery tour and it fascinated him greatly.

Singar was actually seeing the life force aura around all living things and had summoned and made contact with the four elementals to dance around him - fire, air, earth and water.

The party reached their destination near the selected mountain range and laid out their possessions. The elders then held a final short discussion and told the youths that they would wait there for them.

The boys were instructed to remain within the vicinity of the prominent mountain range and to be wary as some of the last straggling bears might be around – those that had not yet moved onto their hibernation destinations near the great river across the next valley.

The boys were required to survive by living off the land for five days and show how they had found and caught game by producing the scalps off the animals they had caught. They were told to split up and live separately, to build shelters and to keep themselves warm with fires using the old method of rubbing sticks together – again, proving this by bringing back some ash to prove that they had successfully completed this task. Then, after wishing them well, the elders sent them on their way.

Singar headed off as far away from the others as he could without making it too obvious. Once alone, he found a sense of peace in this different mountain range environment and began attuning to its unique energy, smells and colours.

It was now late in the day so he sought out a comfortable place to rest for the night. He heard some distant noises as if the other youths were meeting with each other and investigating the terrain, yet he cared not, as he only sought his own solitude and quiet. He had found a sheltered place near a large fir. This location gave good protection from the wind, so he set about making a bed out of the abundant fir needles. He then started to chop down some lower branches to cover himself for the night to keep out of the night chill.

After this was complete, he looked for a clearing in which to start a fire. He had seen it done by his father and had tried to do it a number of times. He had nearly succeeded a few times but just could not get the flames to burst forth from the smouldering wool and fur– maybe this time he could do it.

While there were a few moments of light left, Singar gathered some dry wood and kindling and arranged it all as his father had shown him. He started to rub the two special sticks together which created the heat to ignite the hair of the horse he carried in his pouch. He rubbed and rubbed, yet no smoke came at all.

In disgust, he threw them down, had a sip of water from his small skin water bottle and thought that he must somehow find a pool of water tomorrow to fill his bottle up as well. As his anger subsided, he sensed the small dancing lights around him again and had a thought that maybe they could help him start the fire.

He knelt down and started rubbing again. He then called on the Great Spirit to bless this fire and his dancing lights, to allow the magic of fire to be born. Without a moments delay, smoke and a small flame ignited in his horse hair. This he carefully placed under his small wood pyramid and witnessed a wonderful event – the creation of fire. He had done it! He had finally mastered it! What a joy! What excitement!

The fire kept him spell bound for a long time. He loved its smell and warming atmosphere. He ate some meat strips and dried corn his mother had secretly given him that he had stashed under his cloak. They were not allowed to take any possessions into this trial - only enough to get to the start of the trial - but Singar had kept his ration until now and he realised how famished he truly was. He was also feeling happy with himself and after making sure his fire was safe and low, he pulled the fir branch over himself and fell into a contented sleep.

Dawn came late and presented itself as a dark, overcast misty morning. It had a sort of ominous feel to it, yet Singar was up at the first sign of light. He collected his precious bit of ash that was his evidence of constructing a fire and wrapped it safely.

When he heard soft whistling noises, he knew it was the boys who were on this trial with him and they were trying to find him by following his trail. He instinctively knew it was time to move on.

Quickly he gathered his remaining possessions and covering his tracks as best as possible, quietly moved away in the opposite direction to the whistles and rustling of branches. He felt they were seeking him out and did not like the thought of what they might be up to. He feared the worst so with a great urgency, he moved off as fast as he could.

He was puffing now, as he still sensed them on his trail. He was trying everything to shake them off and nothing was really working, when suddenly he burst into a small clearing and was confronted with a worse fear. A grazing grizzly bear; not a baby bear but a fully grown male grizzly that immediately heard the boy's approach and turned to face him; all seven foot of bear and 500 lbs of deadly muscle.

Singar thought that this was his last day on earth but realised the feeling of wellbeing of that power was within him again. The bear was angry at being disturbed from his breakfast, a tasty berry snack.

He had found the large bush of these juicy delights and was therefore quick to attack and dispatch this small threat to his breakfast. Maybe this thing could be an extra meal as well. The bear closed the gap quickly and was very close to Singar, who was caught between retreating to the one enemy behind him or face another in front of him.

Without warning, a deep harmonious song erupted from Singar's' throat and its primordial sound caught this grizzly in its last stride before a death blow. The bear stopped and simply wondered where this strange melodious sound had come from.

At the same time, the other boys broke through the bush and saw an awe-inspiring sight before them – Singar and the bear in frozen eye contact with Singar making a deep resonant harmonic tone that was mesmerising and entrancing. Slowly, the bear sat down on its haunches and lolled its head from side to side as if trying to shake off this sound but it dazed him and he sat down further to bathe in this pleasant sound that was surrounding him.

Singar had brought forth the resonant tone of nature and planetary life to placate the bear. Then a strange thing happened – nature, in all its forms, came into the clearing and moved towards and around Singar as protection for their friend.

The other boys were so startled by this transformation and sight that they just fled in terror, believing a demon had possessed Singar and it might possess them as well. To make friends with a grizzly was too much. They ran crashing through the undergrowth at great speed, some tripping over and some cutting themselves on the low branches of the trees in an effort to escape the frightful scene in the clearing.

Singar felt this strong powerful force come over him like a wave, as it did at the river. He now felt so tall and strong and yet, at the same time, so humble that this power of Mother Nature could join with him and protect and nurture him. He wept with joy at such an amazing transformation, from a glen of death to a glen of peace; to a bear seemingly sleeping and rocking to and fro, to all the animals frolicking around and birds flying nearby.

He thanked the Great Spirit for saving him and slowly got up continuing the low tone. He then moved further up the mountain to recover from this rather traumatic event. His legs gave out from underneath him after a short period of time and he lay down and cried a little; but then remembered that Braves don't cry so he made a pledge not to cry again. Instead, he sat and thought about what he could do next – still transfixed by this power of energy that flowed through him.

He sensed it had come from two places – the combined nature kingdom spirits and some far distant star or planet that he was having some reoccurring dreams about. He waited for some time bathing in this feeling of empowerment until he felt refreshed enough to continue on.

Singar moved off more confidently now, knowing he was in control and had strong friends or spirits around him. This enabled him to follow a new sense of intuition and feeling as to where to go next, as he felt at peace and at one with everything.

He was following the call of the wild and it guided him now to a small mountain stream providing him with fresh water for his water pouch. The stream was also alive with fish - mountain trout and salmon in great abundance - so a new challenge now loomed to catch one of these prizes in the narrow yet deep mountain stream.

He had been shown once (by the elders) how to creep up to the side of the stream, where the reeds and grasses grew out over the top of the stream, often creating an overhang. The salmon would hide under these overhangs and dart out to catch unsuspecting insects. Singar positioned himself in a perfect location, got out his bow and arrows and waited, knowing that he had to shoot below the fish as the water gave a false angle and position of the fish.

In time, one darted out. Twang went the arrow - a miss. Maybe a fish dinner was not too far off. Then he knew what he must do and so he started his tonal hum again. This permeated the creek and waters all around and salmon came out from under the sides of the stream in a lazy, slow, swimming motion, not darting so fast at all now.

He took steady aim. Singar had practiced this and was quite accurate over short distances, so it all came together for him. The unity of alignment and flow was perfect as an arrow was synchronistically released directly in line with a big slow swimming salmon. He heard a splash and knew that this prize was his.

Singar went in, clothes and all to recover his prize, which had been dazed by the tonal song. With the arrow slowing it further, the fish was easily caught and lifted up to be greeted by a smiling young boy, who thanked the Great Spirit for showing him an easy way to catch fish. Then he prepared a fire like yesterday and cooked the beautiful salmon – what a feast for a starving young brave only 10 summers old.

Singar did not know he could eat as much as he did and his belly felt as though it would burst but finally he felt satisfied. He lay back to look at the painted puffy clouds in the sky and said to himself, "I have learned how to survive off the land. I can now truly become a brave".

He cut slices off the remaining fish and wrapped it up as food for the next few days. He then looked for a resting place that was safe and would give shelter. He also thought that he would not go too far from this location and its abundance of fish as he could live comfortably here until he had to return to the elders in three days time.

Being happy in this decision, Singar saw out the remainder of his trial days in this beautiful locality that was a heaven on earth and where he felt at peace with himself and nature. He had perfected his fishing skills, claiming two more fish scalps. A much fatter Singar reluctantly left this little bit of paradise to reconnect with the elders who had brought him here.

On approaching the elder's camp, he found no one there. The fire had been put out a day or so earlier and there was no sign of the other youths either. He waited the day out, which was the sixth day now and thought that maybe they had moved camp. He wondered what he should do. Should he wait and try to find them here or head back to the main camp. In the end, he decided to wait out one more night and then leave a sign in the dirt near the camp of which direction he was going to head in the morning.

He was up early the next morning and headed off the way the group had originally come. The trail was easy to follow for he remembered various land marks along the way. It was still hard going, yet he felt strong and like a brave now, but mystified as to why no one had waited for him. He thought about the scene with the bear the youths had witnessed and surmised that they had presumed that he was killed by the bear. Surely that was what they thought. Yes, killed and eaten by the bear. Yes, that would explain why they did not come and look for him.

Little did Singar know that the other boys had returned early and recounted their story of the bear to the elders, with Singar singing to it. They all felt that some evil force had overcome him. Maybe Singar thought he was a bear (as this child was different) so they decided to leave him behind and head back to their main camp immediately.

Their thinking was that, if the boy survived, it would be a miracle and if he did not survive they would all accept his death as fate. The boy had caused friction in the camp recently so they surmised that not many would really miss him.

It seemed a cruel and hasty decision by these elders, who were probably acting more out of fear than rationale; but this is what they did.

Chapter 7
Singar's Return from the Dead

So, when Singar finally walked into the camp, he found they were ready to move to their winter lodgings and that there were very few tepees left standing.

He stood in silence at the outskirts of the camp and was amazed that no one came to greet him. People refused to acknowledge him and in fact moved away from him. Most thought him a ghost or some illusion because of the tales they had heard, for surely he must be dead. Some thought that it was the dead spirit of Singar. Yet this strong proud youth stood before them, smiling confidently.

Eventually a quick shuffling of people and voices and signs raised the alarm and Singar's father and the chief quickly approached, as Singar was following protocol and not entering the camp until recognised and invited to enter.

The elders gathered around including the Chief, Two Rivers, and Singar's father to hear Singar's story and ascertain his future in the tribe.

Singar briefly related what had happened, keeping some secrets to himself. He stated that he was able to work with nature to quieten the bear through sound, although what happened was a great surprise to him. He then confirmed that he had brought back evidence of passing all the tests and asked to now be accepted as a brave in learning.

All deliberated for some time about the question of accepting Singar back. His father strongly defended his son, who he was so proud of and explained that he had faced much danger and met it in his own way. He did not run as the boys did and brought back evidence of passing all the tests. He should, therefore, be allowed to be considered for further training.

Much debate took place until fair play finally seemed to win out over fear and the chief said that he would welcome Singar back into the camp. The condition placed on him for this to occur was that he must apply himself fully to further brave training and be ready to face the final 'Brave to Manhood' tests in three summer's time.

What a relief to Singar and his father, who both lit up with big smiles and, as the chief was the final arbitrator, then all must follow his decision. The chief then told Singar's father to come to his tepee after the evening meal to talk.

Kara (his mum) welcomed him back warmly. She rushed off to prepare his meal and attend to her little boy, now three summers old, who was very demanding of her time and love.

It felt good to be back in the company of his people even if they did not understand him. He sensed in time they would. Now he felt he had some respect and privilege in the tribe as he had earned this well and truly through bravery and honesty.

That night, after the evening meal, his father beckoned to him and they moved quietly (as all braves do) to the chief's tepee. Two Rivers and his squaw, Sparrow Fawn, welcomed them both warmly and offered some broth before sitting around the fire and a quiet descended on the group.

Then Two Rivers spoke, "Hawk and Singar, both of you are my bloodline and are from the line of chiefs. You are expected to set examples to our people and follow the law as much as possible, for it is through our customs and laws that we have survived to this day. Singar seems to have inherited this strength. He also appears to possess a power we do not understand. As you know, it seems to frighten those unaccustomed to this strange behaviour. We have had difficult children before and we all work towards accommodating them into our life somewhere.

The Great Spirit has obviously sent Singar to us to help us and maybe test us to see if we are worthy to move onto the stars upon our death. This I do not understand, yet I seek answers to these questions.

As of now, the Great Spirit has not yet shown me through nature and life what role Singar can play in our cycle of life and tribal customs. I looked for signs of what the child's arrival meant. No great calamity has become our tribe. Therefore, I reason that, at this time, he is a good omen and not a bad omen (being the latter would have meant expulsion from the tribe). Now I have spoken, what say you Hawk my son?"

Hawk thought long on what the wise chief had said and chose his words carefully, "I know my son has always been different, this I agree. I have felt in my being that he had a sure part to play in bringing to us a new realisation or understanding of some kind yet this still evades me as well.

He is very good at working with nature and this may bring us ample food when we need it. I also know that because he is different, he is feared and this causes problems for some who see him as a threat to their way of life. I feel if he does his chores and is allocated to one of the elders for further training, then he might be seen to be following our laws and customs. I thank you father for giving him this chance."

The chief said, "Wise words my son", he then looked at Singar and said, "What is this song you sang to the bear Singar?"

Singar had not really been spoken to by the chief as an equal before or given a question to answer. All the chief had ever done in the past was hand out jobs, directions and decisions.

Singar secretly asked the Great Spirit to help him answer this important question and then answered, "I ran into a large male bear and could not move. As it came closer to me I felt this musical song come out of me. It was like a piercing tone or song but it kept coming out of me to quieten the bear and he sat down and went to sleep – that was all." He did not want to mention that he was running away from the other youths at the time.

Both men and Sparrow Fawn just looked at him in awe as this child possessed a power they didn't understand. With a sign, the chief announced that the discussion was over. Singar and Hawk departed the chief's tepee for their own.

A mood of hope now prevailed in both their hearts that some brighter future may be possible for Singar and he may after all blend in and serve a purpose in this Native American tribe.

Singar rejoined the community and applied himself as best he could to the training and duties of a first initiated brave. He was quickly paired with an elder to continue his training.

Initially, he did all he could to please this cranky elder, who was very demanding and worked him very hard. He seemed to mistrust Singar who asked unusual and such strange questions – like 'who put the stars in the sky?' 'Why don't braves and squaws work together more?' 'Why don't we talk to our horses and why do we hit them when they disobey our commands to them?' 'Why are we cruel to other people?' 'Why do we hate our enemies?'

The elder, White Bluff, tried to answer, but after a while he became irritated and refused to answer such ridiculous questions. Singar was therefore none the wiser and decided to ask the Great Spirit instead. He knew that the Great Spirit existed because the tribe believed in it and he was also aware that the spirit had helped him from time to time. He believed that, in time, the Great Spirit would answer his inquisitiveness, but just not at this time.

White Bluff would watch the youth with amazement at how quickly he learned. Yet, somehow, he didn't seem to have his heart and passion in his work and seemed to day dream from time to time. Slowly he came to like Singar and realised that the child was who he was and he could not change him. Maybe he would show him what he knew and this would help.

A slow but strong alliance and friendship developed between the two. One that was both valued and beneficial for both of them – as both were alone in the camp as solitary males. White Bluff had lost his squaw two summers earlier in a tragic accident at the nearby river crossing.

Over the next three summers, White Bluff showed the boy his skills of making weapons, hunting and trapping animals for furs, his stealth at creeping up on prey and how to handle horses. They rode out together periodically to hunt for food and furs, some of which they gave to other families to make covers and coats for warmth and ease of living. White Bluff also talked a lot about the greatest hunt of all, the chase of the buffalo. Singar would soon be taking part in this, his next and last initiation rite of passage into manhood.

Singar fell into a rhythm of life as more summers came and went and he started to feel good about himself. He was enjoying the pleasure of work and doing something well and was proud of his achievements.

He had little time now to lose himself in nature and talk to the small animals. He felt guilty about trapping them and felt he had betrayed them somehow. Deep down, he told them that he was only taking from nature what they needed and no more. He secretly relished lighting the fire at evening suppertime and, when alone, he enjoyed invoking and watching the small dancing lights that would jump into the fire as soon as he started rubbing the burning sticks.

After his bear story had been passed around the camp, he often found himself being pursued by the smaller boys, as if they were waiting for him to do something magic or create another bear to sing to. However, when Singar would not entertain their imagination, they would run off and find entertainment elsewhere.

Singar also ran into the other boys his own age from time to time. They gave him a wide berth as they were now told not to harass him by the chief. He had passed the first initiation tests and now he had earned their respect, which he received, although none sought him out for friendship. This situation was sad for him to accept, as he did not feel he was different.

One day, when they were walking, White Bluff explained how to look for and sense danger signs in nature. These animal signs would alert the observer to the fact that something was not right and that maybe their enemy could be near.

It must be remembered that they still feared the Black Sioux. The Black Sioux were a warring tribe, always trying to steal other tribes' hunting grounds, even though there was plenty of food for everyone. White Bluff said that our tribe had become lackadaisical now, since no battle had occurred for over fifteen summers and last time they fought many braves died on both sides. This story and the views expressed by White Bluff annoyed Singar as he thought that all people lived in harmony with each other.

They then sat and watched a herd of antelope. This game of learning really connected with Singar as he started to see things that he had missed before – like which deer were the watchers for danger and how they took turns to watch for a stray mountain lion. White Bluff also told him that nature provides warnings and messages, although some members of the tribe did not believe this.

Singar felt very close to this old man because they had a common belief in nature and life. He could feel the connection with nature that was sometimes lost through the hustle and bustle of day to day life. Other lessons he taught Singar included that the chance sighting of a fox or coyote could often mean danger and to stay alert and aware of what is around you and seeing an eagle overhead was a sign to look out for what lies ahead and tread wearily on your journey.

Singar slowly came to realise that each animal and bird possessed a trait or mannerism that was typical of their behaviour. Now if an animal made itself obviously known to you, then this was often a message or sign and to take heed. He was delighted with the realisation that he could learn from this and so was his teacher White Bluff.

Chapter 8
Danger Met with Fire and Light

Just before his thirteenth summer trial, Singar and White Bluff were left behind to help care for the tribe whilst a large hunting party headed out to search for the nearest herd of buffalo .They would take what they needed in meat and furs to get them through the winter.

This was difficult for Singar to accept and understand as he did not really relish the idea of shooting such beautiful big animals as the buffalo, but he knew one day he would have to do this. With the large group of Braves away, more work was placed on Singar and White Bluff to get food and meet the camp's daily needs.

One morning, he felt very uneasy and thought that a walk to the nearby stream might be calming for him before starting work. He hoped this might help him feel well again inside and not so on edge.

Approaching the creek he noticed a stray coyote watching him intently from the other side. They both watched each other for some time as if a link was being established; a message imparted and received which confirmed the important ominous feeling he had sensed earlier. The words of White Bluff came flooding back to him, "The coyote is an animal which warns of danger."

He quickly looked all around him for a bear or mountain lion or any other source of danger. He believed in this omen but saw and sensed nothing around him. Yet he found himself on high alert, his senses straining to understand the threat. He went to ground to listen and survey the area and allow his senses to see and pick up what was happening and what could be a danger to him.

Suddenly, he heard a loud scream that sent shivers up his spine –a blood curdling call and whoops and then great shouts of alarm the likes of which he had never heard before.

Singar raced towards the camp and saw smoke rising and heard terrible sounds. When the camp finally came into sight he saw this group of foreign Indians with black feathers in their headdress. They were running through the camp crying out a strange call.

They were hurting his friends with spears and axes – he saw two young braves his age being attacked and not getting up. He felt alone as he had left his bow and arrows back at his tepee, but his feet kept carrying him towards the bloody massacre that was unfolding before him.

As he walked, a power surged through him; an awesome power. He called on his animal friends, the dancing lights and the Great Spirit to help him remove these terrible beings from his people's camp. Then Singar saw White Bluff, his old friend and mentor, struggling with an enemy warrior and others being slaughtered but before he could act he saw his maternal mother scream and fall, Kara was bloodied and hurt.

Singar then let out a tremendous piercing tone that echoed far and wide and created a huge power force that flowed through him and around him. He now walked in a trance state and sought out the enemy braves that had felled his mother and others.

He felt a surge go through him and a strong pulsing energy that left him and went straight through the nearest brave like a lightning bolt that simply blew him apart. He exploded! The combination of sound tone and the dancing lights (elements) created the force that decimated this enemy brave. Singar, still in a trance like state, now sought out the rest of the enemy braves. As they saw him howling and shooting fire, they were initially unsure of the weapon this young brave possessed and just stood transfixed as he moved among them.

Singar had also summoned the collective force of planets, nature, elementals and the universe to help him rid his people of these cruel men. This force could have only be summoned by an enlightened being, totally in tune with the Divine energies and combined nature and elementals energy flows. The force ebbed and flowed through him and responded to his wishes.

With these immense energy sources now at his disposal and a full connection established he became a being of intense light and so he sought out the enemy one by one. The enemy were spell bound. Instead of fleeing, they were mesmerised by the scene of a boy surrounded in light. They went down one after another, ripped apart by the force, seven in all were destroyed.

The remaining ten eventually came to their senses and fled for their lives in a state of fear like they had never known before as all around the earth shook and lightning flashed, from both above and from Singar's hands.

The skies were now cloudy and angry and the enemy were in no doubt that the Great Spirit was not on their side anymore. They fled up the mountain in great haste and headed back to their camp, five days journey away.

When he was sure the danger had definitely passed, Singar wandered back down to the stream in a dazed state of shock and bewilderment. He sought out the solace of the creek and a stand of nurturing white birch trees that provided a warm healing environment for him to recover from his amazing ordeal.

In a state of exhaustion he stumbled and fell amongst the trees and thought, "What have I done?" Although he felt that he had to protect his people, he also felt that he had broken some sacred law of long ago by killing people and that now there would be a reaction or compensation of some sort and this made him feel worse. He even heard an evil voice in his head that chuckled, "Ah! Now Karrindor you are my prisoner on earth and caught up in the Karmic cycle of life and death".

Oh, what a terrible voice it was! What did it mean? He knew that voice and it was one that provoked mistrust. He was now consumed with doubt and fear as the energy force slowly subsided. He felt sad and very, very tired.

He knew that from this moment on, his life would never be the same again. He had given in to anger for the first time; an anger that was uncontrollable. Although he knew he should go and help tend the wounded, he just could not move and fell into a troubled sleep there nestled amongst the birch trees.

It was here the Chief and his father found him. He heard his name being called through the distant mists of time where he had been dreaming of a faraway place of beauty and peace. He wanted to stay there and not return to this violent terrible place...but the sound of his name was clear now as he stirred and moaned and felt hands on him lifting him up and giving him a drink of water.

Then the voice of the chief spoke and Singar stirred to hear Two Rivers say quietly, "You are a true Spirit Child Singar. Thank you for saving our people. I now know why the ancestors have sent you in our midst. You are to be the greatest brave of all times and teach us how to fight our enemies with your powers."

Yet Singar silently and secretly wanted nothing more to do with these powers that cut men to pieces, ripped their flesh apart, killing them instantly. They all walked back to the camp to hear the wailing of women already embracing the grieving ceremonies.

Many of the dead and wounded were being tended to by those who had survived. Singar went with his father to his severely injured mother. He knelt beside her and held her hand. A great sense of sadness came over him as he knew that she would soon pass into the spirit world.

Her love for him was so important for his sanity and his reason for being. He felt so isolated in this community that had always seemed difficult for him. He also found out that his teacher and mentor, White Bluff had died during the skirmish and this hastened the flow of tears down his cheek. With night fall approaching he didn't care about these tears which men were not supposed to allow, for it felt that no one would notice in the dark of camp on this onerous evening.

Once he had no more tears left, he lay down beside his mother and comforted his younger brother who, for the first time, seemed unsure of himself. Soon all fell into a restless sleep, except Hawk, who tended to the moaning Kara throughout the long terrible night.

The morning brought home a realisation that nothing would be the same anymore. Something in Singar had changed: he had felt and used the power of anger and his innocence was no more. Kara had died during the night and Hawk had carried her to a safe resting place in preparation for the great burning of the dead later in the day.

All available men and women gathered wood for a burial pyre. It was upon this heaped wood they placed their beloved ones with their possessions and one by one, each paid their last respects. When the last of the grieving people had passed by the chief lit the burial fire and everyone asked the great spirits to help their beloved ones' souls find peace and a safe and quick journey home to the stars.

Singar's father was deeply saddened and cut himself on his arm as a mark of mourning and respect for the loss of a faithful wife, only then could he move on in life. Hawk then talked to Singar explaining that he, Singar must return to the family tepee and help in the raising of his younger brother.

Singar would also help in meal preparations until Hawk could find a new wife and so a new pattern of life began for Singar. What a blow to Singar to have to care for his annoying and dislikeable little brother.

As the enemy knew where they were, a decision by the chief and elders saw them move camp within two days of the burial of the dead. To leave this fatal place marked the beginning of a new life elsewhere.

Discussions commenced to decide what action would take place to retaliate for this despicable act by the Black Sioux nation. The chief and elders sought out Singar on the second night. They had established camp in a new location at a bend in the river near a steep hillside, which provided some protection and had good views in most directions. Scouts were doing daily rides to set up a safety barrier around the camps new location.

That night Singar found himself seated amongst six elders and the chief. Most of who were not present when the ambush took place for they were off on the hunting expedition. Yet they had heard many reports of how fire and death flew out of Singar's hands.

They now wished to understand this raw force and try to harness it for themselves so that they could somehow use it to inflict a return attack on their enemies. Singar described what he could remember and they quizzed him for hours on how to access the energy. Singar was vague however and kept some secrets such as the dancing lights, his intimate communication process and union ritual to himself. He did not want to do it again or let anyone else access this destructive force. He decided that he would never use this force again to hurt people, only heal and help them.

As a result, the elders were frustrated with Singar for they were none the wiser about how to use this force. However, they gave Singar much respect for his courageous deeds and let him go back to his tepee.

They knew he was still in shock himself and might need some more time to remember things. They did not think the Black Sioux would come back again too soon, after witnessing the firestorm deaths of their fellow braves at the hands of Singar: time was on their side.

Chapter 9
Change of Role for Singar

A boring and dutiful routine settled in for Singar as he virtually became mother to his young brother. At times, he could give him to another squaw who had just given birth, if she had some breast milk left over – but the child always seemed to be hungry and ungrateful for what was being done for him.

Hawk also had little time to continue with Singar's training. He was often with the aging chief and talking with the elders, for it was becoming clear that Hawk would soon become the Chief of the Tribe.

Days faded into moons and eventually into summers, as Singar slowly found a peace within himself again. He had a little more time to ride out on a shared pony that his father owned. He enjoyed the country air and checked on his traps for rabbits and squirrels. These animals would supplement their dinner menu of wild oats, corn and barley.

Because of the attack on the camp, the second initiation rite had been postponed. It was now rumoured to take place at the beginning of the next moon.

There were five young braves who wished to add another feather to their headdress. One feather looked so lonely up top and the second signified that they could also take a wife. When they had accumulated enough furs they could then barter for her from the woman's father.

Urgency gripped Singar and he sought out his father to find out the rules of this final initiation. His father told him that he must ride a horse and shoot a buffalo with bow and arrow. A time was set aside and a spare pony was found for Hawk to demonstrate to Singar the skills necessary for this test. Then he could practice the art of riding the pony using his legs for balance, which would free up his hands for shooting.

As his skill developed, he could shoot an arrow off before having to grip the horse's mane again for balance. It took time and skill to achieve this. A good pony knew what to do; it knew not to get too frightened or turn quickly and throw the rider.

Hawk said that Singar could borrow his pony 'Painted Cloud' for the trial and that he was to practise the full gallop and shooting as much as possible. This training was thoroughly enjoyable for Singar. The pony, however, often seemed to have a mind of its own and, it was quite a few falls later before Singar felt competent in this new skill. He had many bruises to attest to these trials.

Chapter 10
Re-acquaintance with an Old Friend

One day, a great commotion in the camp caught the attention of Singar and he went to investigate. Some of the other braves out on a hunting trip had caught a stray pony that was jumping and whinnying about and although they were slapping it, it would not settle down. Singar hated any cruelty to animals and quickly strode down and asked the braves to stop.

He explained that the horse would not settle while they were beating it. He was quickly confronted by one of the older braves called 'Brave Bow'. He was one of the braves that had chased him towards the bear long ago. He was feeling strong and proud of his capture and was not going to let this upstart young brave claim all the glory from him, so a standoff developed.

Singar felt a sense of power surge in him again and it took all his will power to control it and not use it again. Then everyone realised that the horse was quiet. He had headed straight for Singar and could not be restrained by the two other ropes around his neck. This broke the deadlock between the two boys as they both wondered what had caused the horse to settle down.

Then a most peculiar thing happened; very unusual for a pony! It went up and licked Singar on the face. He then seemed to speak to Singar, "Don't you remember me?"

Singar was amazed as he somehow knew this horse and somehow the horse knew him. A flash of a distant memory came forward of a past pet and dear friend and he knew then that he must have this pony for his own.

Without knowing where the idea came from he said, "I will contest a game of skill for this pony. It knows me and has been sent from the Great Spirit to help me fight our enemies".

A stunned silence prevailed and all felt afraid to take on this claim of Singar's and go against the Great Spirit.

Brave Bow, the one who had caught the pony, said, "True enough, Singar, this horse is different and maybe it belongs to you. But before I hand it over, what will you trade me for it, as our laws dictate this be so."

Singar did not know what he could offer as a trade, so he asked the Great Spirit and the answer came, "I will trade the first killed buffalo on our final initiation trials. You will have first selection of that which suits your needs."

Brave Bow was speechless for a moment. Then he said, "This means that you must be the one to kill the first buffalo – (for only the first killed has all the healing powers transferred to the brave that claims it as a kill.) Well I do accept this as a trade, we will see if you are right Singar!"

Brave Bow stormed off thinking that this crazy horse seemed to have definitely chosen their strange brother Singar as its master, so he might as well give it to him anyway.

As he was walking away he said, "Well, have fun trying to break it in, it is a crazy horse, why it had already tried to bite them all". He used this as an excuse to relinquish ownership of the horse and said that he was glad to get rid of it.

Singar walked off to his tepee with this so-called wild horse meekly following behind, to the amazement of all onlookers. They could only once again shake their heads in amazement and disbelief at what Singar could do with nature.

Singar had an immediate strong bond with the pony and wondered where he had come from. He had many questions about the horse. Had they been together before and was it from that place with beautiful waters, mountains and scenery he visited in his dreams?

He realised that this animal certainly knew him, so he tethered the horse loosely near some long grass and went to find his father and tell him the good news. He also wanted to seek guidance on how to break in this strange horse. "Father, father, I have bartered for a pony recently captured, come quickly and see it."

Hawk was curious to see what Singar had bartered for and quietly hoped it was not his baby brother, as he knew he was a difficult child and a handful for both of them.

The pony was quietly grazing and picked up its ears when he heard them approaching. Upon seeing his master, the pony relaxed but was wary of the other brave. "See him father, isn't he beautiful."

"Yes Singar, a great mountain pony but can you train him in time to ride on the great buffalo trial in fourteen days time?"

Singar asked his father what he needed to do to achieve this. "Trust and firmness is necessary to make the pony understand that you are its master. It is essential. Look after him well and he will generally be faithful to you. Learn to ride with your knees so your hands are free and allow time for the two of you to get used to each other. You may be able to do it in time if he is a smart pony. If it doesn't work out you can still use my pony."

"As well, father," Singar added. "Because Brave Bow actually caught the pony, I offered the first kill from the buffalo initiation trials as payment"

Hawk asked, "Do you think you can do this Singar?" and was assured by Singar nodding and expressing that indeed he thought it was possible. "Well best of luck my son. You will need it. For if you fail to kill first, you will face great ridicule and shame".

With that, the intensive training program began with the pony Singar named 'Manuawh,' which meant 'old friend.'

Hawk had freed him of his duties each afternoon so he could ride and teach the pony to handle the way Indians need them to act and move. He led him around initially with a loose rope around his neck, softly singing to him and getting him used to being led. Then he started to get Manuawh used to having weight on his back by using a blanket and stones as weights.

All this was going very smoothly until on the second day, Singar attempted to hop on Manuawh's back. This triggered some great fear within Manuawh, for he twisted around and tried to unsettle Singer. He went backwards and forwards and then did something very unusual ... he tried to climb a tree. This threw Singar off his back and as Singar watched from the ground in amazement this horse had his front legs up in the tree and was looking up, as if he wanted to climb the tree!

Singar thought maybe he had misnamed him and he should be called Climbing Horse, for he had never before heard of a horse trying to climb a tree. Maybe this horse thought it was some other climbing animal and had become so frightened that it forgot it was a horse. Singar started humming to the horse. Slowly, it settled down and came over to him on the ground and licked him on the face again.

As he felt some pain from the sudden fall he decided not to try again until the following day. He wanted to try talking more to the pony on the way back to camp explaining what he wished them to both achieve. The horse whinnied as if it understood what it was being asked to do.

Singar knew he was running out of time and if he could not start riding the next day, he would have to do the final trials on his father's horse.

If only he and this horse could truly understand each other's mind. As they walked back, a unity of purpose and mind seemed to take place as both walked in harmony and silence to the rhythm and beat of nature. Singar knew something special had happened; a melding of energies and thoughts had occurred somehow and now they had become one team.

He was so eager to start out the next day that he nearly forgot to say goodbye to his father. Hawk was going away for six or seven days and would be returning just prior to the big hunt, which was Singar's final initiation. He quickly caught up with his father and wished him a safe passage.

Hawk was going to the other Chickowa Tribes camp. These were their friends and allies and were once part of their clan. When they became too large, a decision was made by the elders to split into two camps. This would make for easier travel, hunting and general management.

This clan and tribe always remained on one side of the great river and Hawk's tribe remained on the other side. Hawk had told Singar that it was important to keep in contact with their related brothers and sisters and pass on information about the attack on the camp. He would also want to boast about his son's intervention in driving them off with fire sticks and great thunder like noises.

Singar felt proud to be talked about in this way by his father but he did not welcome the attention. He did not wish to be seen as a magical hero but simply as one of the tribe. Singar watched as his father and six other braves headed off into the rising sun and with a wave, they were gone out of sight. They had elected to go on foot because the terrain was not so suitable for ponies.

Singar quickly finished his duties around the family tepee and took his small brother to his grandmother's tepee. She welcomed them both with open arms and asked Singar to stay and talk. Singar made excuses and said he had more work to do.

He left and hurried off to where he had tethered Manuawh – but the lead was severed and the pony was missing. A feeling of despair crept over him as he tried to find a trail and work out what could have happened.

On closer inspection, he saw mountain lion tracks following the pony's tracks, so he quickened his pace and with bow and arrows in hand. He started in pursuit of the hunter and hunted. As he tracked, he also sensed which way to go. It was as if his and Manuawh's minds became connected again, as if his horse was trying to guide him to where he was now.

Singar believed it was lucky that the tether had been loose enough for the pony to break free, or he may have encountered a dead pony instead; a thought that sent great anguish and a shiver through his being.

He had tracked them for some time, when finally he came across an opening in the forest. There was a small pond of seeped water. It was here that he caught a glimpse of Manuawh on the other side of the pond. He sensed Manuawh's uneasiness and distress. The horse's body language told of danger indicating the hunter must still be near. With bow and arrow at the ready, he moved nearer to Manuawh.

Everything then seemed to happen in slow motion: the blur of a large cat, the pony rearing to meet the challenge of the cat's charge and the twang of an arrow that was accurately aimed, as if hitting salmon in a mountain stream. The yellow blur was stunned by a stinging bite in the abdomen and loss of movement as he realised, all too late, that he had become the hunted.

The horse had stopped running away and had started to attack the cat in a strange manner. Then the mountain lion heard another sound; a piercing tone that sent shivers through the cats' spine and drove it into fright, as if some great beast was now chasing him. He fled in painful haste and terror, limping badly.

There was an emotional reunion as Singar and Manuawh were reunited, both locked together in one embrace.

"I thought I had lost you," said Singar. He thought he heard in his head. "It took you long enough to find me, where were you?"

Anyway, all was forgiven. Then Singar threw the rope loosely around the neck of Manuawh and said, "I'm sorry dear friend, may I ride you now?" and with one jump he was on the pony's back.

Slowly, they moved off in unity both feeling the beauty of mutual oneness, understanding and bonding. Manuawh knew which way to go. Singar, delighted with their progress, hummed softly and let him lead them home. They easily negotiated the thick bush countryside before coming out into a cleared plain. Then as a trot quickly turned into a canter with Singar hanging on tightly to his mane, they both moved into a graceful gallop.

A great feeling of freedom embraced them both with the joy and exhilaration of the ride showing on Singar's face as a huge smile. Singar loved every moment of it, the wind on his face and the fantastic feeling of that first gallop which he would remember throughout the rest of his life.

Their skill and riding prowess developed quickly and soon Singar could ride without hands for brief moments. He could now guide the pony with his knees as was necessary in order to shoot an arrow in the great hunt.

The week of his father's departure and separation went very quickly and it was not long before he heard, late one evening, the shouts and greetings of the group returning home.

Singar raced out to greet his father and tell him all the news about the mountain lion and his success with training Manuawh but as he neared his father something made him stop quickly in his tracks. There walking into camp side by side with his father was a strange squaw that he had not met before and instantly he knew, deep inside of him that she was a bad omen, yet somehow he knew he had met this woman somewhere before.

His father seemed very pleased with this woman for he introduced her to everyone as his new wife. Her name was 'Rutten', which stood for messenger or raven, the bird. This new squaw seemed to fill Singar with a strong feeling of uneasiness. However, he thought, at least there would now be a mother to look after his painful younger brother.

Almost overnight, he felt a distancing between himself and his father and he knew who was behind this. He sensed a great evil and innate badness in this new wife – similar to those who had raided the camp two summers ago. The same coldness and selfishness was there.

Since her arrival the liveliness and happiness of the camp seemed to evaporate and disappear, as if some great sponge was sucking out all the goodness, fun and laughter from the camp's activities.

Singar himself felt his own energy and excitement levels getting lower around this woman each day and could not wait to get out of the camp and ride with Manuawh as much as possible.

Chapter 11
Final Initiation Rites

The day finally arrived late in autumn for the youth to manhood trials to begin. These trials had been postponed a further two summers because of fears of other attacks and the danger of splitting up the camp again.

This coincided with the time of year when the buffalo herds were moving south to seek warmer pastures. The young initiates and adult braves would seek them out and gain what food and clothing the tribe needed to see them through the winter.

A high level of excitement was in the camp. Some young women would also be evaluated to see if they could follow the trail of the hunters and locate the kills. They would also help recover the meat and furs and tend to the cooking for the week or two they would all be away.

This would be an arduous test and important trial for these girls as they would be on foot and would need to rely on instincts and the knowledge of life to guide them to the hunter's kill area.

There would be some signs left (an overturned rock, a scrape or mark on the ground, an occasional broken branch) by the adult braves who were going with the youths on the hunting trials. These signs would need to be recognised and understood but would be enough to follow if the young women remained aware and alert. Perhaps most importantly all needed a sense of where the buffalo were to be found.

Singar was up early and busying himself with his chores and his last minute preparations, in particular, checking his bow, arrows and his treasured hunting knife which was given to him by his now departed friend White Bluff.

He thought, "If only White Bluff was alive today he would be here to support me and see my final initiation at an age of fifteen summers".

For it was through White Bluff that he found the confidence, strength of purpose and understanding to use his skills and become a hunter and master of the woods.

Two of those who showed him kindness and love had now been taken from him – his mother, Kara and White Bluff. As well, his father had been distant and aloof and not nearly as approachable as he had been before this new wife arrived.

An uneasy feeling came over Singar, he turned quickly to catch Rutten watching him closely, it was as if she was up to something. She had a smile of success on her face; it was not a nice smile. Singar had a feeling that she was driving a wedge between him and his father. He sensed this strongly and quickly left the tepee without speaking to her.

The ten rode out, seven youths and three older braves to search for the travelling buffalo herds. They left with mixed emotions of pride and a sense of purpose and duty. They were to find food for the clan and to acquit themselves as competent braves, fit to marry and take their place in the tribe. They would then become an integral part of the clan's community.

They travelled through low hills and valleys towards the flatter plains to the west making sure they left subtle signs that only their clan would recognise. They needed to ensure they would not give too much away for any unsuspecting riders that might come their way.

All wore their headdress feathers of achievement and clothes of battle, comfort and warmth. Some wore paint on their forehead for family luck and good fortune, however Singar wore none.

They had been travelling quickly and quietly for five days (with short sleeps) when they sensed the closeness of the buffalo, something that all predators do when they are in-tune with their prey.

After passing over a small river, dust was seen. The lead braves dismounted and led the group to an observation point where they could witness the most unbelievable sight - a sea of moving buffalo across the grassy plains, a truly breathtaking sight.

Never in his life had Singar seen so many animals together in one location. Dust was rising as the buffalo grazed and moved slowly along in groups. Occasionally one would bellow and move nervously back nearer to the safety of the main heard.

Last minute instructions were given by the older braves to ensure each youth knew what to do. Their task was to engage the buffalo and attempt to bring down at least one beast, preferably two. They were shown were to aim to bring down the frightened beast faster. The plan was to shoot where the neck meets the body as this area has a main airway, which will clog up quickly, slowing the beast for a final kill shot. Their arrows were marked to show who shot which beast on the day.

They said a prayer of thanks to the Great Spirit for bringing the buffalo to them and for those that would offer up their lives today as sacrifice for the well being and life of the tribe.

Quietly, they moved further on foot to the last cover of low bush where they would mount their final charge. Singar felt Manuawh's nervousness but reassured him and said to him, "This task must be done". Although they did not like killing animals, it would be just this once.

He also needed Manuawh to work with him because he had to get the first kill to appease his old debt to 'Brave Bow'. He told Manuawh of the agreement he made to first acquire ownership of him. Singar then called on the powers of the Great Spirit, nature and his friends the dancing lights. He then asked them to send a buffalo to him who was ill or unwell and he promised to put it to sleep quickly.

As he felt the power and energy force coming over him, he tuned into the collective spirit of the buffalo and instinctively sensed a better place to shoot. He needed to shoot just behind the front thigh quarter where the heart was located.

Finally, the signal was given and the chase began. Singar and Manuawh were caught slightly by surprise and found themselves left behind at the start of the chase. Singar had been lost in his own world, conversing with nature, so all he could see was dust in front of him as he attempted to gain ground on the riders ahead.

Soon Singar relaxed his directional guidance of the horse and gave Manuawh a loose rein. As he reached full gallop, Manuawh veered off at an angle to the left and so the game of hunted and hunter began. The nearest buffalo saw the other riders coming and they turned and fled towards a valley on an angle away from the hunters. The gap between riders and buffalo was wide and was being bridged too slowly.

The buffalo looked as though they would escape into the nearby valley, when suddenly, out of nowhere, the braves at the lead saw a solitary rider coming in from the left flank at an unbelievable speed. Who was this rider? Surely, he was not one of them! Yet somehow they recognised the pony's colouring. It was Singar, moving in to cut off the group they were chasing!

Manuawh had turned left as soon as Singar released his controlling guidance on him and they had become one cohesive unit of fighting majesty and power. They knew instinctively where to go to find the easiest access to the buffalo herd.

Now they were bearing down on their prey at breakneck speed. They would cut off their escape into the valley and allow the following group to catch up and get within shooting range. The buffalo were mesmerised by the rider who seemed to come out of nowhere. As such, they stalled momentarily in their full gallop of escape. The herd were unsure of where to run next and this indecision was their downfall.

Singar was amongst them in an instant. He slowed slightly now, positioning himself with bow and arrow for a shot. Almost immediately, he saw the old bull running on a parallel course getting closer and closer to him and he knew that this one was his. Within a few lengths he fired his arrow and immediately the beast fell.

The day was over for the old bull who had seen too many winters. Singar felt sad yet elated and quietly thanked the Great Spirit for sending this one to him.

The others now caught up and were engaging and finding their own individual prey. They were bringing them down but not as quickly as Singar had done, for they were chasing the bleeding and frothing animals until they finally dropped.

The excitement of the hunt lasted for a long time and the business of ceremonial claims for the kills was next to be assessed.

All then gravitated across to Singar's one and only kill. He could not find it in himself to kill any more of those majestic beasts. However, the others did not notice this, as he had pretended for a while to continue the hunt.

The old braves looked on in amazement. There was only one arrow sticking out of the huge buffalo, which had great furs fit for a chief, yet maybe the meat would be a bit tough. Great thanks were then said by all for the kills.

Singar walked up to Brave Bow and said out aloud, "The first kill, I give to you brother, as a debt now paid in full. Do you accept this?"

Brave Bow was at first speechless. He then reluctantly acknowledged the debt being fully honoured. He secretly fancied reclaiming ownership of the very fast and beautiful horse, but in the eyes of his peers he had to follow tradition and clan rules and agree. At least he now had the first blood of the kill to give him the great strength of the buffalo spirit and he was satisfied.

They set up camp and did what they could while awaiting the arrival of the young women who were to help with the butchering and making of drays to place the kills on to drag behind the ponies on the way home. All except one of the initiation braves, had claimed a kill according to the marked arrows.

The one who had missed was given another chance the next day to try again. He needed to locate the herd of buffalo and did finally succeed in his quest and rejoined the group two days later, just before the women found them.

It was a beautiful time of collective harmony in purpose and intent at this remote camp. Each worked hard at tasks to prepare the harvest ready for movement back to camp.

There was much excitement and happiness among the young members of the group and sexual urges were also in abundance. The head braves were hard pressed in keeping the young braves and women separated at night. However, an acceptable form of behaviour was maintained as protocol necessitated asking a squaw's father for her hand, before a union of a brave and squaw was allowed. Bonding was not normally approved until both reached the age of 17 summers.

Although Singar was the hero, having brought down the first kill he was not sought out by any of the young women. Inwardly, they each found him exciting and intriguing and sensed the great power and love from him yet they also feared it and couldn't quite understand how to interact with him. They were kind to him and stayed within convention but, because they were now free to marry and start families, they showed more interest in the other initiated braves.

Singar sensed this indifference towards him by the younger women. He finally accepted the fact that he remained different and no one truly understood him. They left three days later for home camp fully laden with meat and furs for the winter.

They were all content and happily making slow but steady progress, when on the second day a band of other Indians were sighted. Both saw each other and watched each other warily. They both then proceeded to move past one another at a safe distance.

Singar was on edge as he sensed great evil from this group. He felt they could have been tracking the women and they were certainly not friendly. They did not seem to have any provisions and there was much concern that they might try to come back and attack them for their bounty. The other men had surely noticed the young women as well and could see them as potential slave possessions.

That night they were all very tense and restless under a half moon. In the end Singar could not stand it anymore and said to Brave Bow quietly, "I go now to see to our safety. Tell the others not to wait for me. Tell no one now."

Brave Bow did exactly as he was told. Even though he still found Singar dislikeable he respected his bravery and this was more important than all else to the men in this tribe.

Singar quietly withdrew pretending he had horse problems. He thought to himself that even though he was not fully accepted, he could at least now prove himself to his father. He also thought that, even if he died a true hero, the tribe would not really miss him, except maybe his father.

Singar went off quietly to seek out the enemy, who he sensed were not far behind. Eventually he found a hideout behind thick brush, an advantage point that allowed viewing access and tried to formulate a plan to confront this group. He had sensed their presence for two days now, but had not mentioned to the others that they were being followed.

He decided that he would again use all his friends and powers to make fearful sounds and confront them. However, in the event they were not thrown off by his howls, he prepared himself with bow and arrows as well.

He was not in his hideout long when he heard the false bird calls. The lead scout came past him not more than three paces away. Then the main group came past, fifteen in total, silently and deadly, all fully armed.

They followed Singar's tribe's tracks in a half moon. Then Singar knew what to do – he mounted Manuawh, who was tethered further away and decided to trail them.

He starting sending thoughts to the enemy that they were in great peril and danger, with the aim of unsettling them. Next, he had nature attack them. Owls and squirrels came out of nowhere and landed on the enemy, creatures of the night responded to Singar's calls and he then joined them with his own blood curdling tone that would send the greatest fear and shivers through any mortal being. He even found himself smiling between calls as he sensed the anxiety and confusion in the attackers ahead until finally the noises of racing feet and hooves gave away the actions of the fleeing enemy – they were in complete panic, confusion and total retreat.

Singar actually then laughed long and hard for the first time in many summers. Although he now had to find and catch up with his clan, he thought he would do it slowly and possibly even stay at a safe distance behind. This way he could act as a rear scout and ensure the safety of his friends on their homeward journey. At the same time, he enjoyed nature, his own company and that of the animals as they all seemed to gather around him each evening. Along with the Great Spirit, they would tell each other great tales of life and the great ruse of frightening away the enemy and helping to save Singar and his tribe.

He loved this time but he also sensed they were close to home, so he quickened his pace. The main party had heard the commotion two nights earlier and feared for Singar's life so they had started out for home as well that night and had also sent a brave ahead to warn the camp of their impending peril.

When Singar finally broke through the last bit of brush near home he saw an amazing sight. A huge line of warriors on horses with war paint were facing him at a distance. It was a standoff for a while as each eyed the other for some time before Singar sang out to them, "It is your brother Singar. I am alone. The enemy have gone".

They then all raced to him and embraced him as a true brave and brother; this was a wonderful feeling of friendship finally for Singar. They were all seeking answers about what had happened. He gave them a brief tale of pretending to be many braves in the night and making a lot of noise, which had caused the enemy to flee. Most of the tribe believed him. However, his father and the Chief realised that Singar had once again carried out some magic, of which they were in awe.

Singar was happy now as he realised that his acceptance within the tribe was growing stronger. Yet he still had to come to terms with his father's new wife, who seemed to bring despair, wherever she went.

Chapter 12
Courting Time

After two more winters and then in the following spring, the courting took place throughout the tribe. All eligible braves sought out mates.

This was a testing time for Singar who was now 17 summers old; for once again acceptance meant finding a mate. It was also an additional incentive for Singar to get away from his father's wife, who seemed to somehow stalk and possess his spirit.

There was an older squaw who was thin and gangly and who had been passed up by all the other braves. She was nearly beyond child bearing age and was not beautiful or pretty in the eyes of the other Indians, yet she was nice to Singar, pleasant and laughed a lot.

Singar sought out his father's advice about soliciting Tara as a wife as he had sensed her glances towards him from time to time. His father forbade this strongly and insisted that he as a future chief, be bonded with a strong rounded squaw who would bear him strong braves and one who was obedient, not like this frivolous old skinny one Singar was considering.

This was a serious setback to Singar's matrimonial plans and he needed to escape from this over bearing tribal custom and conventional requirement.

He went to find solace in the wilderness, the one place he felt at home and at peace with life and with himself. There he felt none of life's pressures and obliging requirements to conform to a rigid pattern of life. In some ways, the tribal life gave him some sense of freedom but not always. In addition, his father's new wife made it so unbearable in camp that he just needed to get away.

He gathered his things and explained to his father that he needed time to himself to think things through to choose a squaw as a wife. This, his father understood and suggested he go with a couple of other braves in a similar predicament.

Alternatively, he could visit their other family tribe where he himself went to procure his new wife. Singar did not verbalise his thoughts but was thinking that if they were all like her at this relation's camp, then he would move in the opposite direction as fast as he could. However, he told his father that this was good advice and he would consider the option.

Singar had loved the times before the new wife arrived, when he had been closer to his father. They had done chores and fun things together... but now his father seemed so distant and so serious with the growing responsibilities of becoming chief that he was no fun anymore.

Hawk was doing more of his fathers' day to day duties as the chief was very old now and would soon go home to their forefathers in the stars. As well part of Hawk seemed to have died with Kara's passing the night after the ambush.

Singar wondered if he would even want to be chief; it was so much responsibility and so much to think about with very little time to yourself. At this time in his growth and understanding, the life of a chief seemed like a lot of work with the many problems and responsibilities it entailed. However, his dilemma was to work out what else he could aspire to that would be acceptable by his father and the tribe.

With all these worries on his mind, he quietly left the camp and headed out with Manuawh to the woods to seek some adventure and excitement. He did not really care where he went, as long as it was away from the camp and his growing list of duties, problems and obligations. Away from a brother who was self centred, noisy and demanding and away from a new mother who lacked any genuine traits of sincerity and had that very conniving smile.

As the camp receded into the distance he started to feel his worries ease and began to focus on the peace and freedom he would find in the woods.

Chapter 13
Singar's Soul Retreat and Revelation Time

Singar rode quietly and slowly off into the wilderness, which was his sanctuary and ally and where he could find peace and contentment. He gave Manuawh a loose rein and even though he tried not to reflect on his duties and responsibilities back at the camp, he found it difficult to let them go and not let them consume him.

He eventually decided to find a sheltered place where he could set up camp and ask for a vision or answer to come to him that would give him some sense of purpose and direction as to what his future role would be.

As the day continued, he found solace in his unity with Manuawh and the daily flow of life in nature that was all around him. Slowly his spirits began to rise again. The eagles soared overhead as if showing him the way to a special place to rest and recover. Later in the day, he discovered a glen close to a creek which had shelter from the winds and ample wood to build a small make shift camp.

It was as if by magic that nature and Manuawh knew what he needed and guided him here to this place of beauty and healing. Singar quickly set a loose tether on Manuawh and removed his meagre provisions – he had only brought enough dried meat for two days, his warm furs for sleeping and his hunting tools and equipment.

After a simple dinner of some fruit he found on the way and some pieces of dried meat, the quiet of the evening descended all around and with the light of the campfire, Singar felt finally at peace again; the demands of the tribe seemed so far away.

He sensed the awakening of the nocturnal animals now scurrying around and investigating what he was doing. They did not consider Singar a threat and came very close to him while he sat very still. Singar once again found contentment and unity in the company of the forest creatures. He hoped that this feeling of contentment would also help provide him with some answers on how to fit into the tribe more cohesively and how to be more openly accepted by the tribe and not feared by them.

Should he take a squaw/wife and become a brave and possibly future chief or should he decide not to take a wife (as none of the camp squaws appeared to be interested in him anyway) and become a recluse as White Bluff had been?

All these nagging questions continued to invade his mind as he tried to relax beside the night campfire. "Ah! What pain and torture they are to me at present". Singar cried "What is my future? Show me what to do, Great Spirit. All these unanswered questions torment me at present."

After a while his mind quietened and he once again felt the presence of the dancing lights as the power of the nature spirits and the Great Spirit embraced him, gently pouring visions and understanding into his head.

He saw all life as a song and dance with all dancing being done to the one song, rhythm, harmony and beat. He saw that each person, animal, plant and tree were part of this majestic symphony and all contributed in some part to this dance and the weave of life. If only each understood the role they were to play.

Upon considering his part and role in the Grand Plan, he saw himself as his tribe's wise man or medicine man offering solutions to life's problems for the people in the tribe and helping the sick. Then he knew what it was he was meant to do and a great smile came over Singar's face. That was enough for the first night, Singar felt more would be shown to him over the next few nights and he finally started to relax and feel more content. He simply lay awake for ages looking at the stars and giving thanks to the Great Spirit for answering some of his nagging questions and doubts and for showing him what his role was to be within the tribe.

The next morning he was up early and ready for a nearby scouting expedition on Manuawh. He preferred to return to the same location tonight as it offered shelter from the prevailing winds. It was a good lookout and had nice energy around it. A close connection to spirit and earth was evident in this location, so unless he found something better, he was looking forward to returning later today.

He soon found water and food. Rabbits and the odd fish were ample for his simple needs and there was also grass nearby for Manuawh. Once again nature had come to his rescue. He eventually decided to return to the same location where he had camped the first night.

The second evening he thought about some more questions and could not wait to see what was revealed to him as he stared into the night campfire.

After the evening meal he relaxed and slowed his breathing. He soon felt calm, relaxed and centred as he once again invoked the dancing lights and sought the wisdom of the Great Spirit to show him the meaning of life.

Soon another vision came to him. He saw troubled people worrying about what could happen in their life and what could go wrong and forgetting how to enjoy the dance and song of life. Life was meant to be easy and fun. It was to be enjoyed with no worries therefore creating more chances and natural opportunities to grow and learn. However, while they worried and doubted all these chances were missed and lost. This brought another great smile to Singar's face as he could see reason, purpose and meaning to life, more than he had even dreamed of before.

When he asked his own questions he saw himself giving chiefs counsel and guidance. He also understood that he would be helping little children see a different perspective on life, encouraging them to not be so serious but more spontaneous and happy again. He now understood that this would also help the parents to become happy again. This helped him realise his role would evolve more and more as the tribe's healer and spiritual guide and mentor, rather than the next chief. The question now was, "How could he convey this role he wanted to play to his tribe and father?"

It went against the beliefs and rules of life that had evolved through many generations of his tribe. His tribe's survival was based on the tried and tested old ways involving gallant braves who did brave deeds to save the tribe or get food for the clan.

However, there was little wisdom in these rules, traditions and stories except for the one story concerning survival and guidance relating to where their tribe came from a long time ago. This tale told that the tribe apparently came south from a frozen wasteland and had to negotiate lakes as big as seas in rafts of wood to finally arrive in this fertile valley between its great mountain ranges. Yet little of that former life and culture had been remembered or recorded in song or story, it was as if they did not want to remember what it was like before.

Maybe the tribe needed a new dreaming song to embrace the future and once again give purpose and meaning to life?

Finally, Singar fell asleep on the second night with many more questions than answers on his mind. He was reasonably content in the knowledge that he had some answers and that he would find a way to tell his father what role he would like to take in the tribe.

On the third night a great force rumbled through the distant hills as Singar was completing his meal of fish, berries and nuts. This sent shock waves through his whole being as he immediately sensed great danger to his tribe and family. However, even though a great unease had come over him, being a moonless night he elected to stay where he was and not journey home.

He really wished to see what visions the Great Spirit had in store for him that night. It was difficult to settle as he knew it wasn't thunder he heard but what could it have been? He felt it was some strange foreboding.

His scattered thoughts took a long time to settle but he eventually invoked the dancing lights and Great Spirit to show him more on the meaning of life.

Soon great shafts of light were shown to him descending down to earth with each light awakening those souls asleep or lost in life. Some however refused to dance with these new beacons of light and shunned them instead. Some tried to hide from them as they were fixed in the old ways. Some of the people were just not comfortable with the new song, dance and weave of life.

The visions went on and showed him that eventually most embraced these new shafts of light and new happier ways of existing but Singar would once again be challenged to introduce the people to this new way of thinking and believing. He knew he would face much opposition before it was widely accepted, but he accepted the challenge and so he started to formulate ideas and stories that could maybe help him with this quest to get others to understand.

Long into the night while there was this disquiet in the land he sought out ways to embrace the meaning of life and tell it through stories or song. He formulated a story which involved a little lost brave who had lost something and when he asked the Great Spirit and Nature where it may be found he would be shown or told how to relocate it.

It was a fantasy tale yet opened up the inquisitive and intuitive minds of the children to what was possible and what they may create or achieve in life.

What if the little lost brave had lost his wisdom and looked and looked everywhere for it, under a tree, under a boulder and even in a hole underground but still he couldn't find it.

The story would show that as the brave was not kind or helpful and was too selfish and greedy, his heart would remain locked to what he sought. The story would then go on to show that once he started to help others and share his food and belongings then the wisdom would pour into his heart, mind and soul – so his lost wisdom wasn't really lost at all but locked inside his heart and body all along.

Once Singar realised that he could make up a story for most aspects of life concerning the little brave, he finally fell into a fitful sleep.

Chapter 14
A Great Catastrophe

Singar awoke to a grey day and not the usual nature sounds at all. Everything seemed quiet and eerie. The animals were watchful and sensed something was wrong. Singar remembered that last night there was a great noise and rumble so he quickly prepared for departure.

Then he heard the sound again deep within mother earth, a painful grinding noise as if huge boulders were being rubbed together. Then the shaking of the ground which this time stopped as suddenly as it began.

Singar sensed that the Great Earth Mother seemed troubled and restless and wondered what had caused this discontent within her being. His heart song told him that something was amiss and he must hurry back to his tribe to see if all was well in his family's campsite. It did not take long to pack up his belongings, find Manuawh and start out back towards his home at a fast pace.

He already knew something had happened at the tribe's camp but could only speculate what it could be and what danger would be present.

Late in the evening he reached the vicinity of his camp's domain and saw much damage from the fallen trees and dislodged boulders from the sides of the ridges.

From a distance he saw what had happened, part of the mountain side had collapsed. It would have slid down very close to where the camp had relocated to provide protection from the winds and enemy. All was not well here. As he neared the camp he then heard the wailing of grieving female voices getting louder.

Singar saw the damage, quickly dismounted and ran toward the chaos to help. The smell of death was in the air and emotional cries were heard from those in grief and shock. Fallen tepee's and smashed effects littered the campsite; it was a sight of great devastation. Some were aware of his return but most were too busy trying to find missing loved ones. The land slide had swallowed half of the tepees and camps' inhabitants and much had been washed away down the ravine toward the river. What a disaster! What a mess!

The survivors worked late into the night retrieving bodies until they dropped from exhaustion. Nevertheless, Singar kept looking for signs of life under the rubble, for his father, new step mother and the old chief were still missing. Fortunately, his brother had been in another tepee with a brave his own age planning hunting trips and so was spared.

When he eventually found his dead family he cried out in great pain and anguish at once again losing those dear to him. He wept as he moved them to a safe place from which to carry out the traditional burial rites the following day.

Singar continued to help his tribe search for other lost loved ones and he was frantically looking for the old chief as he had not sighted him anywhere. He was advised after enquiring about him that he had gone over to the spirit world whilst Singar had been away. This heightened his sadness and he felt a huge burden of grief as he tried to get some sleep near the camp fire that had been kept burning this black night.

The next day once all the tribes' people had been accounted for, the burial process began. Because of the large numbers of dead it was decided to once again have a burning pyre.

It was tiring work for the already exhausted tribe members, gathering wood from dead trees and building up the platform of the burning pyre, on which to lay all the bodies. They were then covered with their possessions and smaller branches. Late on the second day, a senior elder lit the fire and the official wailing started anew.

This time all joined in and the sound ebbed and flowed through each soul as the pain of loss wrapped itself around every heart. The wailing continued until no more tears flowed and the time came to comfort each other with food and drink and to think about instilling order once again to the tribe.

Chapter 15
New Leadership

On the third day the tribes people came together to look for new leadership. As they were still shocked, angry and grieving, the discussions were lively and heated.

Some proposed Singar be appointed the new chief, yet others opposed this saying he had not a wife or yet proven his ability to lead and make decisions.

Singar then asked to address the council, for he had listened to all the talk and it seemed to be going nowhere. He felt he had a good option to present to the gathering. "Fellow brothers, braves and families, I know we are saddened at the loss of our fathers and mothers yet we must come to a decision and not bicker anymore as it is pointless. May I suggest that as a trial, a council of seven braves be appointed to lead our tribe in all matters and make all important decisions.

I wish to be part of this council as an equal and not as chief and have equal voting power as any others. I also propose that two women who are wise in the ways of our ancestry sit on the council. This would be a trial for two moons in which it will give us time to think about a new chief".

At this point Singar did not wish to mention that he did not really want to be the chief, with all the responsibilities and duties that went with that position.

All were dumb founded at this most unusual request, which was so different from the ways of old, yet in principal, it sounded so logical.

"Who is with me on this plan? Show by signs of fists", Singar said.

Initially only four agreed. After further discussion, eventually all came to see the merit in Singar's proposal. Those against him did not want to give in to his plan too easily for that would look like they were supporting him. Eventually the proposal was passed by a majority show of hands and the task of soliciting who would sit on the council began.

Then Singar surprised them once again by suggesting that the tribe's elders be part of the council with him. Once again they all couldn't agree on this. They needed wise people who were best suited to carry out decision making on behalf of the tribe.

In the end it was simply easier to accept Singar's idea than debate who held the most wisdom. The elders were then voted in as the tribe's new interim council of wisdom. This was the first time women had been invited to partake in the decisions of the tribe and a new precedent was created by this clan's evolving new medicine man.

The council worked very well and they followed Singar's advice often as he seemed to have the wisdom of the Great Spirit flowing through him.

Before a vote each member was given a chance to express his/her opinion without interruption and then a second time around if they had any further input into the discussion. Then they voted. If the voting was undecided a time out was convened for all to talk to family and friends and contemplate. They would then convene the next day until a strong majority or unanimous decision was reached.

The process of decision making for the tribe progressed very smoothly with most feeling happy with the new procedures being implemented. However, there was still a group that was pushing hard to reinstate the old system of a chief making all the final decisions for the tribe.

This persisted even when Singar spoke out about how exhausted his father seemed to be most of the time and how he had not been happy in life because of his work load. Secretly Singar felt it had been the new wife's manner and ways which were mostly to blame for this change in his father's demeanour but spoke not of it.

As the time approached for another decision to be made Singar was ready with a new proposal, which would result in another major change to the old ways of the tribe.

He introduced the new proposal to the council that stated that any member of the tribe could address the council with concerns or worries they felt important for the tribe's best interest. After much discussion, the council of elders voted and it was accepted unanimously.

This was a great coup as most of the tribe members actually came to express their individual feelings in relation to why a chief was necessary and whom they thought should be the chief. Hence, a lot of the unrest about the chief issue seemed to abate as individual tribal members were given the opportunity to communicate their feelings at the council gathering.

Three summers passed with the council of elders admirably performing all the duties and decision making that the Chief once carried out.

Then finally came the time for the discussion of who would be the new chief, who would also sit on the governing council. Prior to this time Singar had sought out his younger brother, who, although he ate and slept with since the landslide – he rarely conversed with, other than the mundane platitudes of the day.

His younger brother had passed both the initiation tests with ease and was a brave to be reckoned with as he had all the loud actions and bravery mannerisms that would suit a chief under the old system.

Yet the people had proven to be comfortable with the new laws and discussion based council and some did not wish it to be removed.

One day Singar spoke to his younger brother quietly and said, "I wish to hear your counsel on a few ideas."

It was here that Singar planted the seed that he did not wish to be chief and that he felt his younger brother Hook would be best suited. Singar told his brother that he understood he was a favourite amongst the tribe and held all the strong characteristics of a leader and that Singar himself was not popular enough.

Singar's truthful confession took Hook by surprise yet he controlled himself and took his time before answering. "Yes I can see why you choose me as I am more like our people and more accepted by them than you are. It would be a wise decision."

This comment stung Singar deeply but he tried not to let it show. He thanked his brother for his opinion but asked that he keep this conversation to himself until the council had been told.

Singar knew immediately Hook would not be able to keep his mouth shut and in no time all would hear that he was to be the new chief. This suited Singar for he could point out to the council that his younger brother was too boastful and arrogant to be a chief just yet. While he himself did not wish to be chief, he felt that it would be in the best interest of the clan that the council should keep running the tribe for the time being. The people would see the merit in this outcome for quietly Singar felt great concern for the tribe if his younger brother was ever elected as chief, for he was headstrong and trouble often followed him.

Six moons had passed when the council convened once again to discuss the topic of chief as well as other minor matters. The council of elders had grown in confidence and wisdom by this time and had slowly begun to trust Singar and his ways, as he seemed a natural wise man and leader. In this forum he had introduced many important new ideas that were generally endorsed by the Council so when he made his proposal at this gathering all saw the amazing wisdom that was within this quiet, reserved young brave Singar.

Singar proposed that his brother be nominated chief after he took a squaw and showed that he could make decisions that were wise and considerate of everyone.

Singar would act as his mentor and guide and report to the council when he felt that his brother had achieved the appropriate calmness, strength and leadership qualities he needed to understand the council's ways and to show the necessary growth and wisdom to allow the council to continue to function and not consider disbanding it.

Some of the elders were disappointed in Singar's refusal to accept the nomination as chief, yet others understood that not all wanted him as their leader because of their fear and lack of understanding. Therefore it was an easy solution to come up with and by agreeing to the proposal all council members stayed in their positions of influence, which they now enjoyed. It also solved the dilemma of who was to be the next chief.

Hook was of the line of chiefs so he was eligible to be nominated. This big discussion affecting the whole tribe was then opened up to all the clan to gauge their reaction.

Singar was elated by the group discussions at this time, which reflected little opposition to him being the new chief, if he wished to accept the nomination. Many had voiced their support towards selecting Singar; however, others wished to return to the old ways and would need more convincing.

Singar's proposal to nominate his brother, whilst keeping him under supervision until he was more mature, was a solution that everyone could agree to. Hook could then be coached and learn to show more restraint than his current brash, loud ways, which many realised mirrored the ways of chiefdom from yesteryear. That is, often the loudest or strongest male generally became the leader.

Everyone was happy to accept Hook under the new terms. Hook on the other hand was furious at being deceived and felt Singar was to blame for his predicament at not being given full reign as chief, so he proceeded to take out all his frustrations on Singar by being nasty and refusing to talk to him at all. His bitterness and anger was obvious through many outbursts towards Singar and this was witnessed by many.

More summers past with Hook refusing to conform to the council's decision of learning the new ways of governing in the tribe. It all came to a head one day when Hook publicly challenged Singar to a duel to prove he was ready for leadership. He knew that by doing so, Singar could not refuse, as a challenge to a duel was a very serious matter in tribal law and needed to be honoured and accepted.

The only satisfaction Singar had was that as the one challenged he could choose the form of combat and weapons. This too was the law and custom of the tribe and as Singar knew he was better on a horse than off, he chose the lance or long spear on horseback as their method of combat.

Both practiced using the long spear and became accustomed at manoeuvring it on horseback which wasn't the usual technique. This type of spear was normally used for chasing mountain lion or bear on foot as the spears were about six foot long with a stone point at one end and small feathers and decorations along the shaft and very difficult to use on horseback.

Singar would ride one handed and steer Manuawh his horse with the other while he practiced piercing a scrub tree as he rode past.

How did it come to this he wondered? What would a final showdown between two brothers from the line of chiefs prove?

Singar felt that he would rather die than allow this pompous, loud, selfish brother of his lead the tribe as chief and so he sought to discredit him and embarrass him somehow which would show the people that he was not worthy of their respect and fidelity.

Singar also felt it would be a backward step if Hook won as the people would cease their progress. He sought guidance and support from the great Spirit for this forthcoming clash as he felt strongly in his conviction to oppose Hooks claim to be chief at this time, if ever.

The day of the contest finally arrived. Singar was 23 summers old now and Hook had turned 16. It was fine after a few days of rain and instinctively Singar felt this was a good omen and quietly asked the Great Spirit for help and protection in the contest. He believed that the Great Spirit would let the best and most worthy man win.

At the appointed time both riders rode out to either end of a long clearing with everyone in the tribe waiting and watching. All wished to witness this spectacle between two great warriors.

Many strange stories had been heard about Singar and the people were wondering if he would use this magic on his opponent today.

Both braves were dressed in war paint and had their feathers of initiation on their head. An eerie quiet crept over the valley as if the entire world was watching with bated breath.

Both now eyed off each other and waited, seeing who would charge first. Hook could wait no more and charged with lance held high. Singar did likewise, both hurtling towards the other.

When he was half way towards his opponent Singar did a remarkable thing. He rotated his lance so the blunt end was facing his opponent and the sharp end was tucked tightly under his right arm, locked in by a leather strap he had made to secure the lance.

His intention was to bunt his opponent off his horse at the same time realising he would need to dodge Hooks lance when thrown at close range. The entire crowd witnessed this move by Singar and cried out in despair for they thought he was going to his death this way.

They were only five arms length away when Hooks arm went back. Singar quickly veered left and ducked to enable him to go down his opponents left side. However, the spear went fast and true and struck

Singar on the upper right arm. It would surely have killed him if he had not turned left at the last moment.

The pain was piercing, but as his lance was braced in a sling, he could still manage to hold on to it and steady himself. At the last moment he struck Hook perfectly on his chest, which dismounted him totally. Hook fell flat on the earth winded and stunned, unmoving. Singar pulled out the remainder of the broken lance that had struck his arm. It left a nasty hole and as the blood started to flow he knew he didn't have much time before he himself would faint. He dismounted and rotated his spear once again.

Singar walked over to his brother and placed the point over his heart and said loudly, "Do you yield? Now answer!" All was quiet and then he challenged again pushing the point stronger into the flesh of Hooks chest. "Do you yield?"

He then heard a faint "Yes" which was what he wanted all to hear and witness, as this was an acknowledgement that the contest for the role of chief was over for his little brother.

Chapter 16
Singar's Brush with Death

Singar quickly went to his tepee to stem the bleeding with a tourniquet. He tied some cord around the shoulder socket and packed the gaping wound with dry moss to stop the flow. One of the elders then came to him to tend his wound. The elders plan was to loosen the band regularly to try to save the arm, but he was doubtful it would work.

Singar then passed out and dreamed of another world of beauty, love and friendship. He drifted in and out of consciousness for days due to the large loss of blood. It was doubtful he would survive. Death visited him on a few occasions and he had felt light and without pain, then he would find himself back in his pain filled body.

Days and nights came and went until finally, on the fourteenth day his eyes opened. He saw a familiar face come into focus as he tried to grasp where he was and what had happened.

She was Tara, the only woman in the tribe who had ever showed any attraction and interest in Singar. She had been tasked to keep the levels of broth and water up to Singar.

It was a miracle that he had survived with such a bad fracture and deep wound. He noticed that he had a bandage of bark over the wound and healing paste around the wound itself.

He had many questions for Tara, including who had been caring for him. She told him that she had been, so he thanked her for her time and help and immediately asked about his younger brother. Tara told him that Hook had left the same day as the contest in great disgrace and embarrassment – as he had failed in his quest to beat Singar in combat and had not been seen since.

Singar also enquired as to the welfare of his faithful horse Manuawh to which Tara informed him that his pony was safe and had been well cared for. This partially satisfied Singar as to what had transpired since his long sleep and considering his wounds, he thought he probably owed his life to Tara's healing ways. She was smiling proudly at him and sensed his gratitude towards her. Both savoured the moment of joy and happiness in Singar's' survival.

The word quickly passed around that Singar was awake and more arrived in his tepee. There were now many faces looking at Singar with smiles all around for he had won their admiration and support. From the contest he had also shown them compassion and respect for each other and they had come to finally understand Singar and accept him as one of their own.

During the time it took for him to recover from his almost fatal experience and get his strength back of the many who came to see him and wish him well were the children of the camp. He welcomed these children gladly. It was during this time that Singar started telling them stories about the 'Little lost Brave' that always seemed to lose everything. These stories became very popular with the children as the deeper meaning of the stories reached the very centre of their heart and soul.

He even found that some of the elders would sit, listen and often nod their heads in understanding to these simple but remarkable stories.

Tara continued to tend to Singar's needs until he could finally manage by himself. Tara had never bonded with another and being much older than Singar, she had accepted that she would remain a single squaw helping around the camp. She shared a tepee with another elderly couple.

As Singar slowly regained his strength, he and Tara established a mutual growing enjoyment and happiness in communicating and discussing life together. Both found they had similar views and interests particularly regarding their love of animals, nature and life. After a short courtship Tara came to live with Singar and a blossoming romance grew and flourished, with much laughter emanating from their tepee at any time night or day.

One day Singar and Tara (watched by many friends) officially said their vows to each other beside the river under a beautiful stand of birch trees. As Tara's mother and father had died in the great avalanche, the elderly brave from the tepee she had once shared gave his blessing to their union. Happiness and love had finally come to Singar and Tara.

The miracle of creation happened to Tara a summer after their bonding, a baby was conceived and nine moons later a healthy boy was born.

What a magical event this was for everyone. It was quite unbelievable as Tara was considered by many to be well past her child-bearing age. This made the birth all the more special and profound. Many believed Singar had used some form of nature magic on Tara to create this special child.

He was a happy baby who was loved and admired by all, particularly Tara who never expected to ever conceive a child.

The child was given the name 'Wise Owl' as when he was born an owl was heard hooting loudly nearby and it continued to do so throughout the birthing process.

Tara and Singar both found their roles and purpose in life; helping their people reconnect to the rhythm and meaning of life. Tara was good at healing the sick with herbs and natures elements and she also had a gift in healing sick animals and birds. Tara and

Singar both complemented each other in many aspects of life.

Singar did recover but he never regained full use of his right arm, so instead of becoming chief, 'Singar the Wise' became one of the first medicine men of the Indian nation. He changed their perspective on life and as a result, they prospered and were a very happy, contented tribe.

Throughout Indian history, all remembered this wise brave who told stories and reconnected them to the ways of nature, life and death as one cycle and rhythm of communal existence.

Wise Owl grew up a great leader and lived up to his chosen name. He became Chief at an early age and continued the traditions his father had introduced. The council of elders became the corner stone of wisdom, judgement and decision making throughout the Indian culture for a very long time.

A new dance and song of life then came into being, with Singar and Tara being models for this new happier communal existence. This in turn allowed a new dreaming to begin, as the people were once again receptive to receiving the wisdom and guidance from above.

Singar was very pleased. He and Tara lived out the remainder of their days helping the Indian people understand a greater truth to life.

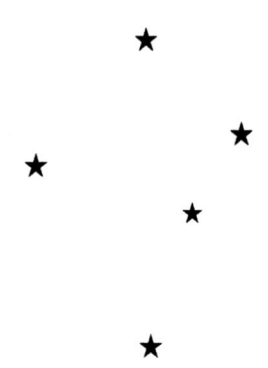

About the Author

Ross was a pilot in the Royal Australian Air Force for over twenty years. During his flying career he was captain of a large military aircraft at the young age of twenty one years. He went on to become a flying instructor and test-pilot. His love of flying and the freedom of the skies has seen him embrace and love other fictional stories such as 'Star Wars' and in turn has motivated him to create his own journey through the stars.

He is now semi-retired and lives with his wife and animals on their retreat nestled in the Snowy Mountains area of New South Wales, Australia.

Life Skills Australia

We publish material that is inspirational, life changing and positive and most of our titles are written by independent authors - consequently, many of our sales are via "word of mouth". We need an army of people worldwide to help us spread the word about the great messages contained within these books.

If you would like to help us then visit our website at www.lifeskillsaustralia.com and click on the "Affiliates" link.

Life Skills
AUSTRALIA

www.lifeskillsaustralia.com
info@lifeskillsaustralia.com